ANTHONY MASTERS

WICKED

 ORCHARD BOOKS

To Robina, as ever, the light that doesn't go out

ORCHARD BOOKS
96 Leonard Street, London EC2A 4XD
Orchard Books Australia
14 Mars Road, Lane Cove, NSW 2066
First published in Great Britain in 1997
First paperback publication 1997
This edition published in 2000
Text © Anthony Masters 1997
The right of Anthony Masters to be identified as the author of this
work has been asserted by him in accordance with the
Copyright, Designs and Patents Act, 1988.
A CIP catalogue record for this book is available from the British Library.
ISBN 1 84121 732 8
1 3 5 7 9 10 8 6 4 2
Printed in Great Britain

Chapter One

JOSH GROPED his way out of sleep, immediately remembering that the twins had a secret. Naturally, it was one he didn't share. He was always being left out now. But he was getting used to that, so why was he so scared?

He stumbled out of bed and pulled back the curtains, gazing at the broad sweep of the Thames at the bottom of the garden. The river was a reassuring sight, calm and familiar, a slight haze rising from the surface in the early summer morning. The Thames was an old friend, always changing yet always the same, unlike the twins. They had a secret and they were afraid.

Jack and Tom seemed much closer than before, cutting their younger brother Josh out completely. The way they looked at each other, whispered in their room, exchanged uneasy glances, seemed so obvious that he couldn't understand why Mum and Dad hadn't started to ask questions. But then they were so wrapped up in being busy, in getting edgy with each other, that

Josh reckoned it wasn't so surprising they hadn't noticed. It couldn't be his imagination though. It had to be for real. Worse still, Josh felt that he had lost Jack. They had always been so close. Tom was different, much more self-contained, but Jack had always been protective of Josh – as if he needed to fight someone else's battles as well as his own. Then, just a week ago, Jack had seemed to withdraw, quite suddenly, as though he had gone into a room and slammed the door.

Several times Josh had been on the point of asking the twins what was going on, but at the last moment he couldn't find the words, as if he was being bounced off an invisible wall that was protecting his brothers. As a result he began to watch them carefully and noticed they were watching each other in a way they had never done before – rather as if something nasty was creeping up on them and it was a competition as to who was going to cry out first. It was a weird feeling but Josh was sure he was right. The twins were scared and Josh was scared for them. What had they done?

The morning was so suffocatingly hot that when Josh emerged from the river he wanted to dive straight back in again. The heat haze still shimmered over the water and the surface looked as if it was steaming.

Jack and Tom had already put up the stumps; they were passionate about cricket and would practise together for hours, completely immersed in developing

2

their skills. Josh wasn't much good at the game, and he supposed that was why the twins rarely let him play, although that didn't stop him asking. It wasn't that he liked cricket – in fact he hated the game – but he wanted to be with the twins. The closer he got to them, the quicker he might learn what was bothering them so much.

"Can I play?" he yelled hopefully.

"We're practising for the team," Jack said irritably. "And we don't take passengers."

Josh winced, the hurt darting about inside him. The twins were fifteen. Josh was twelve and the age gap had always made a difference, but now that Jack and Tom didn't seem to want him around any longer the summer holidays yawned ahead, a desolate waste with nothing to do.

Their father, Richard Tyler, was Head of English at the local comprehensive his three sons attended, while their mother, Anna, was a social worker. The Tylers were always busy, but this summer they were busier than ever, organising a conference about urban violence, leaving Jack, Tom and Josh to have "fun in the sun" as their mother expressed it.

But they weren't having fun at all.

"I'll field," said Josh, trying to please Jack. If he was useful, they might let him stay, but if he wasn't, if he made the mistakes he usually did, he knew what would happen.

Jack was the more dominant of the twins. He was

short and dark and muscular, with a wilful nature, and had much the same natural authority as his father, which meant they often clashed. Although he shrugged it off, Josh knew that Jack was upset by these confrontations; he was always trying to get closer to Dad, but Dad usually managed to back away.

Tom was quieter and rather more thoughtful. Last week, when he and Josh had been playing cards, he had suddenly said, "I thought twins were meant to understand each other even if they're not identical. Sometimes I don't even know Jack." At the time Josh had found Tom's words incomprehensible; now he kept remembering them. Tom was usually so reserved. If only Josh had been able to ask him what he had meant. But he had held back. Yet again.

"I'll field," Josh repeated.

"All right," said Tom absently. He was a dedicated sportsman – even more so than Jack – but was often more willing to give his younger brother a chance, in a casual sort of way.

Jack scowled. "If the ball goes in the river," he snarled, "you're for it. Understand?"

Josh nodded apprehensively.

The twins hadn't always excluded him like this, but that seemed a long time ago, well before the "change", as Josh was beginning to call the fear that had come into the twins' eyes. Of course, in reality, the change had only come a short while ago, but already it seemed like an eternity. Josh tried to remember when he had first noticed the difference in them. Was it when Jack had been whispering to the Fletcher boys on the telephone and had banged the receiver down as Josh came into the hall? Was it when Tom, placid Tom, had hurled a tub of ice cream across the kitchen table at Jack? Or was it when Jack had locked himself into the bedroom all one morning, shutting out his twin, who had hammered on the door and then walked away self-consciously as Josh had run up the stairs?

Josh positioned himself by the river bank, trying to concentrate hard to blot out the disturbing thoughts, ready to catch the precious cricket ball, although he didn't have a lot of faith in his ability to do so. His coordination was poor and sport inevitably posed a problem.

"Watch the ball," yelled Jack.

"I am," Josh called back defensively.

Jack picked up the ball and ran down the wide area of sun-scorched grass. Then he came to a stumbling halt, pursued by a Golden Labrador who wanted a different kind of game.

Jack frowned as Josh gave an involuntary laugh, and then waited impatiently while the owner tried to call his dog off.

"Paddy!" he shouted. "Paddy! Come here at once."

But the dog only jumped up, anxious to get at the ball.

"Can't you see I'm bowling?" Jack shouted angrily.

"And can't you see I'm taking my dog for a walk,"

yelled the man, turning belligerent. "This isn't a cricket pitch, you know. It's a public right of way."

"Call him off," ordered Jack, rather like Dad might have done. "He's messing up our game."

"Paddy!" yelled the man. "Come away. You don't know where that lad's been."

Eventually the Golden Labrador reluctantly loped over to join his master. Waiting resentfully until they were both out of range, Jack bowled a savage yorker at his brother.

Sweat was running into Josh's eyes. The grass was parched, the branches of the trees still, the leaves looking as if they were made from hot metal. An occasional motorboat droned up and down the river and the tarmac was melting on the path that snaked away from the bank towards the rusty swings. He had often been an outsider, even before the twins had shared this secret. As an entity, they left him out, had always done so, because Tom and Jack were sufficient to each other. It was only Jack who had made the effort, vainly trying to teach him to have an eye for a ball, to tackle properly in rugby, to shoot in football. Once he had even warned a boy at school to stop bullying Josh. Maybe he'd suddenly given up on him because he was such a wimp. Could he be *that* disappointed in him? The twins didn't really need him of course. But, on the other hand, they *all* needed Mum and Dad. That was the last link they had – the absence of their always busy parents.

It was mid-week, and the Thames was largely deserted. A muted traffic hum came from the road nearby and Josh suddenly felt sleepy, his concentration lapsing badly, as it so often did.

"Catch!"

The command came as a shock, and Josh gazed up helplessly at the sky, the hard round cricket ball glimmering in the hazy sunlight, insubstantial in the white heat. He ran backwards and waited, trembling hands cupped, eyes straining for a glimpse of it.

The ball seemed to wink contemptuously, glimmer and then go straight through his fingers.

"Pratt!" yelled Jack furiously.

"Idiot!" bellowed Tom.

Still dazzled by the sun, Josh began to run after the ball, but it was going too fast and fell with a plop into the river, floating for a few seconds and then sinking rapidly, as if it was made of lead.

"Sorry," muttered Josh. He knew he was going to be in big trouble now.

"Sorry?" Jack was suddenly beside him, his face bright red and his whole body shaking with a rage that seemed too big for such a small incident. "You're going to be sorry all right."

Tom ran up, looking apprehensive, and Josh felt his eyelids pricking.

"You'll pay for that ball." Jack's eyes burned into his.

"Go to hell," shouted Josh with angry bravado. Dodging round his brother, he ran away down the towpath, determined they wouldn't see the tears he was trying to hold back.

"You're a rabbit," shouted the school PE instructor in Josh's mind. "What are you?"

Josh ran on, hugging his misery to him, a rejected victim yet again. Was it never going to end?

Josh often came to the overgrown island on the Thames if he was unhappy or wanted to think or both. It had a folly shaped like a miniature temple, and Josh had always been fascinated by the old building, so small and perfect but purely ornamental. He stood on the river bank and stared at it thoughtfully. He felt hurt and bewildered rather than angry. Jack could be impatient, even scoffing, but never as cruel as this.

Josh sat down on the burnt grass and glanced over his shoulder; the twins were nowhere to be seen and he assumed they'd gone back inside the house, an old rambling vicarage their parents had bought and converted ten years ago. Behind him was Henley Bridge and downstream was Hambledon Lock.

Josh remembered how last summer Jack and he had once gone out in a rubber dinghy on their own. They had paddled round the island while Josh had made up ghost stories in daylight. That was quite a feat of the imagination, to create a spectre in blazing sunlight. But he had succeeded, telling his brother about a young girl who had walked into the river and drowned herself because she was frightened of her stepmother. When he had finished, Jack had given him an admiring glance which sent shivers of pleasure down Josh's spine. "That's not bad," he remembered Jack saying. "Not bad at all."

A family of swans floated gently by and then scattered as an eight rowed past, their blades dipping in and out of the water, their wake golden in the fierce sunlight.

Soon the Thames was peaceful again, the surface glassy, rippling slightly at the bank with tiny lapping sounds, and the swans glided out of the protection of the bank, heading up towards the lock.

The miniature temple looked cool and welcoming, and on impulse Josh decided to swim across to it. Officially no one was allowed to land as the island was privately owned, but Josh went over there frequently and had never met a soul. It was his own territory, a hideaway, a private sanctuary.

Making sure he was unobserved, Josh slid into the water, and the Thames took him in its cool and silky embrace as he swam slowly towards the island.

Chapter Two

PUSHING HIS way through tall grasses and dry and brittle bushes, Josh reached the steps of the temple. Sitting down in the shade of its pillars, he checked his waterproof watch. It was just after one, and he knew Jack and Tom would be tucking into the cold lunch their mother had left out for them. They would probably eat his share, Josh thought miserably. Well, let them. He didn't feel hungry anyway. He'd rather sit here and think about the secret – the secret that must be behind Jack's behaviour.

Josh wondered if there had been some big row with Dad that he didn't know about. Jack certainly hadn't been getting on with him recently but that was nothing new. They were just too similar, often falling out almost for the sake of it. Only last night Josh remembered Dad bawling, "Go up to your room. I'm not putting up with that kind of lip. What's got into you?"

Jack had run up the stairs and slammed the door while Mum had turned on Dad. "Why don't you *talk* to him? Is that the way you treat your kids at school?"

An argument had broken out and Josh and Tom went to play cards in the kitchen.

"What's up with Jack?" Josh had demanded.

"Nothing," Tom had replied quietly, and something about the way he said it prevented Josh from probing.

Josh wished that Mum and Dad spent more time at home. Maybe that would solve all this miserable secrecy, mean that the twins had someone to talk to. That's what happened in most families, wasn't it? You could always go to your parents and tell them what you were worried about. Then Josh realised he was being stupid; most of his friends at school *never* confided in their parents. It was uncool. But it would be nice to have the chance. Mum and Dad seemed even busier nowadays, as if it was a competition between them, as if they didn't want to have any time left to think. The last thought was surprising, and Josh felt a sudden shock. Why didn't his parents want to have any time to think? Were they unhappy too, like the twins? Unhappy with each other? Unhappy with him?

Ten minutes later Josh swam back to the bank, shook himself and hurried up the towpath towards the house. He was hungry now and Temple Island had once again soothed him. It was as if he had stepped off the planet for a while.

His gloom returned, however, as he thought of the long weeks of the holiday stretching ahead of him.

What was he going to do? Why had he turned down Michael's camping offer or the adventure training course with Tim? Was it because he had wanted to stay at home with his brothers? To see if Jack was going to be good to him again?

He remembered Mum saying, "This is an expensive house to keep up on our salaries, but look at its position. I mean – it's a year-round holiday in itself." Josh wasn't so sure. You could get too used to a place.

As he neared home, Josh remembered the twins had also refused invitations, but there was a good reason in their case: Paul and David Fletcher and the old sailing dinghy they had been given. Would the four of them go off together and leave him behind? Probably. Josh's misery deepened. Why had he dropped that catch? But why had Jack been so angry with him? The mystery remained and his head hurt thinking about it.

Josh heard the angry gasping sounds as he opened the wicket gate by the river and walked up through the garden. Then there was a burst of shouting and swearing. Were his brothers being attacked? Josh broke into a run, his heart pounding, the panic surging.

As he approached the house the shouting became louder, punctuated by groans and gasps and thumps. Josh tried to call out, but his voice seemed frozen and he couldn't bring out a word.

The noise was coming from behind the shrubbery by the garage, near the lane that led to the main road.

Had the twins caught a burglar, or even a gang of them?

Plucking up all his courage, Josh ran round the laurel hedge.

Jack and Tom were rolling about on the ground, kicking and punching, both covered in sweat, their faces tight with exhaustion and with an alien enmity in their eyes. Josh had never seen his brothers fighting like this before.

"Stop!" he shouted feebly, but Jack and Tom took no notice, rolling over and over in the rank dry grass.

"Stop!" Josh repeated frantically, but they only fought each other the harder, the early afternoon sun filtering through the trees, casting its searing light on their locked-together fury.

"Stop it!" Josh screamed for the third time, and then threw himself on the twins, trying to prise them apart physically but only succeeding in rolling over with them, their combined weight crushing him painfully.

Eventually it was Tom who brought the struggle to an end, breaking away from Jack while Josh clung to him. For a moment he thought his brother was going to hit him, but instead Jack pushed Josh away and stood up, taking in great shuddering gasps of air, the sweat running in streams down his tanned cheeks.

Josh struggled to his feet. "What the hell do you think you're doing?" he demanded.

"None of your business," rasped Jack.

13

"You never fight."

"It was only for fun," gasped Tom.

"Fun? Call that fun?"

"Let's go upstairs," said Jack, staring hard and meaningfully at Tom. "Get some peace."

"Peace?" Josh was horrified. "Are you going to fight up there? Mum will be furious."

"Shut up!" Jack turned to his twin. "You coming?"

Tom followed his brother in silence, leaving Josh shocked and amazed, hardly able to believe what had happened.

Surely they wouldn't fight again, he thought, not in the attic they shared. The twins loved the huge space, big enough to contain a table-tennis table as well as wall-to-wall posters.

Tom's favourite rock stars were on two of the walls, and Jack had covered the others with racing cars and trophy-hung drivers. The attic was their own special world. They *couldn't* destroy it.

"Wait!" Josh yelled as the twins limped towards the big gabled Victorian house with its conservatory and outbuildings.

"What do you want?" Tom turned back to him reluctantly.

"I want to know what's going on."

"Nothing."

"Is it a secret?"

Jack darted Josh a venomous look. "Push off," he said threateningly.

"There *is* something going on," Josh muttered.

"Listen." Jack spoke slowly but forcefully, his eyes locked into his younger brother's. "There's *nothing* going on."

Josh sat miserably in the kitchen, picking at the corned-beef sandwiches that his mother had left out for them and that his brothers had left untouched. He could hear them moving about upstairs, going in and out of the bathroom.

Josh pushed the sandwiches away. Why did she always leave out corned beef? He was fed up with the stuff and when he looked in the cupboard he could see the shop-bought apple pies that tasted of sweet and gooey cardboard. They sat there, daring him to eat them. Yet again.

Chapter Three

TEARS PRICKED at the back of Josh's eyes, but as they trickled down his face he wiped them away fiercely.

There was silence from upstairs now. The twins must still be in the attic, but what were they doing?

Suddenly, he felt he hardly knew them – as if they were strangers. He tried to remember them as they had been – Tom, kind but efficient and self-contained; brave Jack, fiery temperament yet always ready to reach out, protect, support. But who were they now? Had his brothers changed for ever as they hugged the secret between them? He loved Jack and Tom, however much they had excluded him, not these aliens who had suddenly moved into his home, trying to destroy each other for some reason he couldn't fathom and then locking themselves away so silently in the attic.

Josh made up his mind. He would creep up the stairs and listen, despite the fact that he was afraid they might catch him spying on them.

Of course they probably weren't silent, but Josh

knew he wouldn't be able to hear what they were saying unless he was right outside their door.

The house seemed unnaturally quiet, the silence broken only by the sideboard clock with its loud, hollow tick.

Josh got up, walked cautiously into the hallway and then began to tread as softly as he could up the first flight of stairs, which was solid and thickly carpeted.

When he reached the first landing he paused, listening to the ticking of the clock downstairs, horribly aware of the silence closing in on him like a suffocating blanket. Josh felt he could hardly breathe, his whole body heavy and unresponsive, rather as if he was slowly being buried alive.

He walked on up the landing towards the un-carpeted wooden stairs that led to the attic and paused again, waiting, listening, but hearing nothing.

Slowly, he began to climb, cautiously inching one foot up at a time, praying that the creaking wouldn't give him away. For a while nothing happened, and then a great wooden groan seemed to resound all over the house. Josh shut his eyes against the awful sound, waiting for Jack to come thundering out of the attic, but the eerie silence was unbroken.

Then the whispering began, and Josh listened intently, picking up the odd word here and there but unable to make any sense out of them. Then Tom raised his voice for the first time.

"We've got to tell someone. We can't leave him there. We just—"

"Shut up," hissed Jack. "He'll hear."

Josh stood outside the door, not daring to move, straining his ears. Despite the heat, he shivered. His own house seemed to have become enemy territory. What did Tom mean - "We've got to tell someone. We can't leave him there."?

Josh listened to what seemed like silence. Then he had a terrible thought. Did the twins know he was outside? Were they about to open the door and pounce on him?

He tried to move but couldn't. A mysterious force held him on the wooden stairs, his feet locked into the boards.

A sudden blast of rock music as one of the twins switched on their CD player made him start so badly that he almost cried out, but as soon as Josh realised what it was his feet became unrooted. Relief flooded him as he ran softly down to the landing and into his own room.

He lay on the bed, exhausted. The heat wasn't so intense on this side of the house and his bedroom was cool and dim with the curtains still half closed. Outside he could hear the drone of a motorboat and the shouted instructions of a cox. In his mind he heard Tom's voice repeating over and over again, "We've got to tell someone. We can't leave him there. We've got to tell someone. We can't leave him there." What did he mean? Tell about what? And who was being left?

Tom had always been the more straightforward of his brothers. Not exactly the most honest, but the one who saw things more simply. Josh remembered watching Jack and Tom playing in a school football match. The referee had made Jack offside and, naturally, he had disputed the decision. Afterwards, when they had all been discussing the situation, Tom had said the referee's decision was final. Jack had once again disagreed. "He was wrong," he had pronounced angrily.

"But in the *game* you have to accept he's right," snapped Tom. "It's in the rules of the game. You've got to obey them."

"Why?" Jack had asked, quite mildly for him but very positively. "You can't always play by the rules. Not if they're unfair to you."

The discussion had become an argument and dragged on. But Josh knew that Jack was unshakeable in his conviction. What *was* this secret? Had more rules been broken?

An abrupt knock on the door suddenly interrupted his repetitive thoughts.

"Who is it?"

"Jack."

"What do you want?"

"To talk."

Reluctantly, Josh got up and opened the door. He had to ask Jack what it all meant.

"What do you want to talk about?" Josh asked uncertainly, but Jack didn't seem to want to come to the point. Neither could Josh summon up enough courage to put the terrible question.

"You're still wearing your swimming trunks." Jack sounded shocked.

"It's so hot."

"You've been lying on your bed in damp swimming trunks –"

"They're dry," Josh said defensively.

"Mum will be furious." Jack hesitated. "Look, I'm sorry I was so angry. I was tired." The words came out in a rush.

"Tired?" Josh was incredulous.

"I don't know why." Jack seemed to find the explanation as inadequate as Josh did, but then he hurried on. "You can play cricket with us. If you want."

Josh was morosely silent.

"If you like."

There was a long silence.

"That fight. It started in fun. Kind of got out of hand."

"You never fight," said Josh doggedly.

"We did then, but it doesn't *mean* anything."

They stared at each other.

"These things happen."

"Yes?"

"They don't *mean* anything," Jack repeated fiercely.

20

Josh still couldn't ask the question. His mouth was so dry that he couldn't speak at all and there was another long, uncomfortable silence. After a while his brother went back upstairs to the attic.

Josh suddenly felt cold. He flung back the curtains, letting in the sunlight and gazing down at the river, basking in the comforting heat. The house was oppressive. It was full of secrets and he felt as if it had put a curse on him, preventing him from asking the very question that might break the secrecy and let the light in again.

Chapter Four

THAT EVENING, Richard and Anna Tyler came home full of their conference, falling into a long discussion that completely excluded the three boys.

As their parents talked, Josh noticed Jack watching his father cautiously, while Tom kept his eyes on the floor, occasionally gazing up at his brother.

Eventually the twins changed into their smart clothes and went to a youth club disco in Henley while Josh, with nothing better to do, watched TV in the sitting room, Tom's voice beginning to repeat itself again in his mind until Josh had a grinding headache.

Eventually his mother joined him, her thoughts obviously elsewhere, staring through the television, while his father tapped away at his computer in the study.

Anna Tyler sighed and Josh looked up at her, their eyes meeting for the first time in what seemed a long while.

"You OK?" she asked.

He nodded.

Josh had always been closer to his mother than his father, but nowadays even she seemed to be getting remote.

When he was younger, he and Mum used to row up to the lock in an old rowing boat that was now kept in one of the outhouses and hadn't been used in years. In fact it was Mum who had first explored Temple Island with him. When she had seen the ivy-shrouded NO LANDING sign, she had turned to Josh with a glint in her eye.

"I know we shouldn't but ..."

With conspiratorial daring they had moored the boat under an overhanging willow tree and crept ashore. It had been autumn and a chilly wind had been blowing off the river but, almost magically, a patch of mellow sunlight had illuminated the temple's cracked stone steps.

"Ancient sunlight," Mum muttered, brushing back a lock of Josh's hair.

They had sat very still, protected by a screen of dense blackthorn, guilty, furtive, but happy to be together.

Now she was gazing at him searchingly. "Not getting bored?"

She had the same blonde hair as Josh, the same long frame, the same uncertainty. Why was she trying to compete with Dad? Wasn't that yet another secret?

"A bit."

She sighed again, and Josh realised that despite all

her preoccupation she actually did care about him, and a rush of warmth filled him like the sunlight when he had opened the curtains of his room that afternoon.

"I should never have taken on this conference. Your father was so keen to—"

"It doesn't matter." But Josh knew that it did.

"Of course, the twins have got each other." She sounded as if she was thinking aloud. Then she asked abruptly, "Why didn't you take up any of those offers from your friends?"

"There were only two," he replied morosely.

"Two's enough." She gave him a rather weary smile, as if she thought they might have an argument. "At least that gives you a choice."

"You had a choice," he said without thinking.

"*Sorry?*" She flushed, and then the colour receded, leaving her face white and strained.

Josh shook his head, hardly understanding what he had said, surprised at the way it had come out, as if the anger had been stored in the back of his mind and had somehow leaked out.

"It doesn't matter," he repeated.

"But it does." Mum was giving him all her attention now, for the first time in a long while, and Josh pressed home his advantage.

"Did you *have* to do this conference? With Dad? I mean – we've hardly seen you all term. You're always so busy and now you're busy again." His voice was flat.

"Yes." So was hers. "But I still haven't seen much of your father either." She suddenly stood up. "We must spend more time together, Josh."

"The twins don't want me." He realised his voice was betraying him – that she would guess he was holding back the tears. But they had suddenly come, caught him unawares, just like everything else round him.

His mother shrugged impatiently, wanting to take a no-nonsense approach. "They're going through adolescence. It isn't easy." Her grinding common sense swamped him, but Josh was determined not to drown in it. He fought back, although he knew he sounded childish.

"It's not fair. Jack used to play with me. We did all kinds of – he used to *show* me things."

"He will again."

"Can't *you* see he's changed?"

"He's darn difficult, but so are most adolescents."

Josh wished she wouldn't use that stupid word. It sounded as alien and hostile as the secret. His mother looked at him and tried harder.

"Tom's always been more stable. Jack's the emotional one. You're like him in that." She paused and then spoke as if to herself. "Jack's strong though. Always has to be in control. Of himself, too. I wish I could get through to him."

"So do I," muttered Josh, but she didn't seem to have heard.

He knew she wanted to stop talking now, to get away from him and the painful things he might be saying.

"Let's take the boat out soon," he pleaded, and saw her face soften, as if she was recalling a distant land called the past.

"Do you still go to the island?"

"Sometimes."

"On your own?"

"Yes."

They gazed at each other blankly and then his mother gave Josh a bright smile.

"We'll take a picnic soon," she promised. "Just the two of us." She paused. "The twins are so moody nowadays. It can't be much fun for you." Mum sounded as if she thought it was her fault.

That night Josh lay awake for a long time and then slept restlessly, finally falling into a confused dream world, dominated by his brothers. Daubed with war paint, they were hardly recognisable, but he knew it was them. They picked up painted swords and ran at each other, shouting in a language Josh had never heard before.

The battle was long and intense, but neither of the twins seemed to be winning. Eventually Jack struck his brother with one of the swords and Tom went down saying, "We'll have to tell someone. Whatever you do, in the end we'll *have* to tell someone."

Suddenly a trumpet sounded and large wooden gates opened to reveal his parents sitting at a table, rapidly folding papers and then putting them into sealed envelopes marked TOP SECRET. They didn't look up as Jack hit Tom again with his painted wooden sword.

Then the dream abruptly faded and Josh woke to harsh sunlight.

Later that morning, the Fletchers arrived to work on the sailing dinghy. Although it belonged to them, all five boys had been working on the boat for some time. She was stored in the Tylers' outhouse and the repairs were nearly complete.

Josh had been designated the dogsbody, at everyone's beck and call, and this morning he carried out his tasks humbly, without thinking.

Paul Fletcher was fourteen, slightly running to fat, a rather clownish daredevil. He was immature, given to teasing, but always took care it didn't rebound on him. His younger brother David was much less outgoing, somehow a natural victim. He and Josh had always got on well; being the youngest was a common bond.

Both the Fletcher boys wore their light brown hair long; Paul had tied his back in a ponytail but David let his hang down on to his shoulders. Their mother had left the family years ago and they lived a haphazard life with their father, Tim Fletcher, a potter.

The sailing dinghy, the *Moorhen*, had been beautiful

once, broad-beamed and ideal for river sailing. She was clinker-built, with jib, mainsail and a centreboard, but she had been rotting in a boathouse for a long time and needed a good deal of restoration. Now she was almost finished, and today they had decided to relaunch her.

As the five of them pushed and pulled the dinghy down the slipway opposite the house, Josh wondered if he would ever have the courage to confront Jack. He felt frozen inside, unable to ask the question that would solve everything. After all, maybe the secret wasn't so bad. But he still couldn't bring himself to ask.

Although Jack was showing Josh an impatient kindness, he could sense that he was preoccupied, and when he glanced at Paul and David he could see they were wary, and Paul kept watching Jack as if anxious to take his lead from him. David, however, seemed the opposite, intent on avoiding Jack's gaze. Could whatever was troubling his twin brothers also be troubling the Fletchers? Surely there was an underlying tension in them as they talked determinedly about the dinghy. The conversation seemed forced, and Josh wondered if they were darting glances at each other that were probing, untrusting. Was all this his imagination? Or were the Fletchers involved in the secret as well?

David soon came under criticism from the older boys, and Josh felt an unworthy sense of security, as if he was getting close to the other three at David's expense.

"Watch what you're doing, Dave."

"You're pushing the wrong way."

"Get a grip on the bow, can't you?"

As a result, David became increasingly flustered, his long hair getting into his eyes and even winding itself round one of the stays.

Josh thought he could see tears in his friend's eyes and felt bad.

At last the dinghy was afloat and, as she didn't seem to be leaking, everyone's mood improved and David was released from his role as victim.

"We should have a launching ceremony," said Tom as they all five stood knee-deep in the water, still admiring the results of their handiwork.

"I name you *Moorhen*," said Paul, splashing water on her bow. "Good luck to all who sail in you."

Once they were in the dinghy and Jack had got the sails up, the crew began to relax. The morning was not so intensely hot as the previous day and there was a breeze that made the little boat bounce along, the water scudding underneath her bow.

Jack, who had done a sailing course, was at the tiller, looking commanding as usual, while Paul and Tom sat on either side. David took the jib sheet, while Josh was still at the ready to be everybody's slave, too anxious to be accepted to be annoyed at his lowly role.

The breeze increased slightly and Jack bellowed, "Ready about." The mainsail and jib came over smoothly and the *Moorhen* started to make wide tacks over a broad stretch of the Thames.

"She goes great," Josh yelled at Jack, who smiled graciously, as if acknowledging praise from a galley slave.

Later, the wind shifted and the dinghy went on to a run, the strengthening breeze behind her, her mainsail and jib filled with its momentum as she headed towards Hambledon Lock.

"We'll have to get the sail down if we're going through," Jack shouted.

"We'll look right pratts if we capsize," warned Paul. Despite the fact that he was quick to make other people the butt of his jokes, Paul was always ready to protect himself.

Jack sighed. "We're not going to do that," he said reassuringly. "Not if you do *exactly* what I tell you," he added patronisingly.

He began to give a stream of impatient instructions which Paul and Tom carried out with the minimum of fuss, hardly rocking the dinghy at all. David and Josh looked on, both irritated at this display of zombie-like capability.

Eventually, now under bare masts, the *Moorhen* was bobbing up and down in the gently lapping water, waiting for the lock gates to open, and the five sat silently, enjoying the freedom of being on the wide, empty river.

Then Josh saw David staring at the track that ran towards the lock from the main road. At first he seemed just curious. Then he began to shake.

Chapter Five

THE POLICE car was travelling slowly, dust rising in spirals, a magpie wheeling above it.

Josh looked over his shoulder at Jack and caught just a hint of the threatening stare he was levelling at David before he quickly turned it into a false grin. Paul shifted his position, his weight making the dinghy rock, while Tom glanced at him uneasily.

"Someone doing the drugs run," Paul said brightly. He often made trite comments like that, his clown's mask well in position.

The police car drew to a halt and an officer got out, leaning over the white-painted railings to speak to the lock keeper. Josh strained his ears, but couldn't hear what either of them was saying because of the chugging of a nearby motorboat. Again he glanced back, this time seeing beads of perspiration standing out on Jack's forehead. What was going on? Why had David been shaking? "We've got to tell someone. We can't just leave him there," said Tom's voice in Josh's head.

The policeman turned casually towards them,

stretching and yawning. Momentarily Jack's gaze rested on David, but there was no expression on his face now.

For a second the policeman appeared to study the crew of the *Moorhen*, then he walked casually back to the car. He got in and sat talking to his companion as the lock gates slowly began to open.

"Come on," snapped Tom, fitting the oars in the rowlocks and turning to Josh. "You take one – and I'll have the other."

They pulled together until they were inside the slimy, weed-hung gates.

"Grab the chain," commanded Jack.

But Josh was already hanging on to it, still puzzling, still wondering.

As the gates closed and the water level began to drop, he could just see the police car driving away. Once again Josh glanced around at the others, but the expressions on their faces were inscrutable.

"Watch out for the weir," said Jack. "We don't want to get too near that or we'll be shipwrecked. Tom and Josh can row us out of range."

As they rowed the *Moorhen* out of the lock, Josh could hear the roaring of the weir. The familiar sight was threatening, the water cascading down, a foaming torrent, making a huge turbulent lake in which canoeists often tested their skills. This morning there was no one there and the lashing foam sprayed out hungrily towards the dinghy as Josh and Tom pulled hard to bring it out of the water's reach.

Once they were clear of the white water, Jack ordered David to put up the mainsail. He began fumblingly, to the accompaniment of derisive comments from Tom and Paul, and as a result did much worse, until the sail stuck and wouldn't go up any further.

"You idiot," said Paul unfeelingly, watching his brother contemptuously.

"Pratt," commented Tom as David continued to struggle.

"Don't keep yelling at him," said Josh suddenly, his friendship for David finally beating his desire to be one of the group. "He'll never get it right."

"I couldn't agree more." Jack was surprisingly sympathetic. "Shut up, both of you. Now start again, David, and take it slowly."

Patiently he talked him through the process, putting the dinghy into the wind again, and soon David had the sail up. He leant on the bow breathing heavily, amazed that he had succeeded.

"Well done," said Jack quietly and David looked relieved, but it flashed through Josh's mind that his praise contained a measure of control.

At lunchtime, half a mile further down the river, the crew of the *Moorhen* pulled into the bank and ate their sandwiches. But the underlying tension was still there, making everyone loud and silly, even laughing at Paul's pathetic jokes.

"Why don't we camp out for a night?" Josh said

suddenly. "We could take a couple of tents."

Jack nodded. "Why not?" But he didn't seem very interested.

"We could take some booze," said Paul.

"You ought to lay off the beer," observed Tom uneasily. "That's why you've got a paunch."

But Paul was unabashed. "I was thinking of taking some of Dad's cider."

"You'll have to ask him." David was censorious.

"Who said I wasn't going to?" There was a scornful note in Paul's voice.

"Can I come?" asked Josh, afraid that he was not going to be included, determined to strike now while he was on better terms with them.

"I don't see why not," Jack replied, slightly grudgingly.

"Great!" Josh was pleased. The closer he got to them the more he might learn.

"You'll have to do the cooking," said Paul provocatively.

"No, he won't." Jack was brisk. "We'll all take turns."

But when Josh looked up at him gratefully, his brother was staring across the river, a hand shielding his eyes from the sunlight. With a sense of shock, Josh realised that Jack's hand was shaking.

The *Moorhen* tacked on. Josh felt detached from reality, seeing the passing life on the river bank as a series of unfinished stories: the woman with a pram stacked full of apples, the vicar hurrying towards a moored cruiser, the little girl crying at a garden gate, the policeman watching them intently.

"Ready about," said Jack sharply, as if waking from a trance.

The *Moorhen* turned back to the lock, and when they reached it Tom brought the sails down. Later Paul put them up again, making a terrific mess of it all, much to everyone's delight, particularly David's.

On the last long stretch there seemed to be little wind and the *Moorhen*'s sails filled only fitfully. She made increasingly slow progress until the breeze died away altogether and the dinghy drifted under some overhanging trees and came to a bobbing halt.

While the others tried to pole her off, Josh stared down into the dark water, probed by tree roots, long sinewy fingers that felt their way down to the depths. Anything could lie at the bottom of the river, he thought. Last year Josh remembered seeing the bloated carcass of a sheep under the surface. Maybe there were human corpses too. What about the school teacher who had disappeared? They had dragged the river for Mrs Laidlaw but had never found her. Could she be down there, trapped under the tree roots, bloated and swollen like the sheep, huge eyes staring up from her watery grave? Huge eyes in the white wet suet of her...

"Josh?"

"Yeah?"

Jack was gazing down at him curiously, his eyes guarded.

"You're shivering."

"Someone just walked over my grave."

"*What?*"

"It's a saying."

"I know it is. I thought you were catching cold." Jack sounded slightly irritated again.

"On a day like this?"

"Why not?" laughed Paul. "Perhaps you're going down with swamp fever."

Josh shrugged.

As the breeze came back, Tom pushed off the bank with an oar and the *Moorhen*'s sails filled again, taking her away from the dark shadows of the trees. "Do you still swim out there?" he asked curiously as the dinghy sailed past Temple Island.

"Sometimes," said Josh shortly.

"What for?" asked Paul.

"Just for fun."

"Fun?"

"It's like a jungle," said Josh inadequately, feeling childish.

"And you're Jungle Josh, are you?" asked Paul.

"Someone should clean up that island," said David. "It looks a real mess."

"If they did it wouldn't be a jungle any more," explained Tom.

"Let's land," suggested Jack.

"No." Tom was adamant.

"Why not?" demanded Paul.

"It's Josh's place."

"I bet you he just sits there and thinks about girls." Paul grinned maliciously.

"Shut up!" said Jack. For a moment Josh felt the glorious return of Jack's protection. Then it seemed to disappear, like the early morning mist from the river.

As the *Moorhen* approached the final reach, the sun began to set in a crimson blaze, turning the river a dark purple and the trees a strange and vivid orange. The river doesn't seem real any more, Josh thought. A threat hung in the still evening air.

Chapter Six

THAT NIGHT Josh heard whispering again, but this time it was coming from his parents' bedroom, next door to his own. The whispering seemed angry and then he distinctly heard his mother say, "We can't go on like this. It's affecting the children." She had forgotten to whisper now.

"Rubbish."

"They *know* we're at loggerheads."

"You're imagining things."

"Haven't you seen how the twins are behaving?" she asked. "How miserable Josh is?"

"Nonsense."

"You're so complacent. Why don't you ever give us any time? Can't you see how far you've grown from Jack – from them all?"

"Keep your voice down," snapped his father.

They began to whisper again and Josh closed his eyes against his parents' anger, but he couldn't sleep. He tossed and turned for a long time before he eventually drifted off into a troubled doze, only to dream again, this time of Mrs Laidlaw rising from her watery grave, wagging an accusing finger at him.

At breakfast the Tyler family were determinedly cheerful. Josh listened to Jack proposing the sailing and camping idea and Dad was quick to be encouraging.

"Sounds like a great idea, but you won't go camping on private land, will you?"

"No chance," said Jack, sounding overemphatic and also slightly hostile, as if he resented not being trusted. "We're going to make the trip today, while the weather lasts."

"And Josh is on board, is he?" asked Mum rather hesitantly.

"You bet," said Tom.

"Wish I could come with you – instead of sitting in a stuffy conference hall." Richard Tyler briskly buttered toast and added a generous helping of marmalade.

"It's air-conditioned," Mum insisted, but Dad wasn't rising to the bait.

"Do you remember how we used to take that old skiff down to Marlow?"

"We used to sleep in barns, didn't we?"

We sound like a happy family, thought Josh, but aren't we just playing at being one? The room seemed to darken.

*

The crew of the *Moorhen* started the voyage boisterously, as if they had to fill the air with noise. Paul told

39

corny jokes and Josh laughed at them while the others groaned. Jack whistled at girls on the bank, never relinquishing the tiller, despite numerous requests, while even Tom became more forthcoming and told them how one of his teachers, a Mr Ferris, had fallen for Amanda Rackham, a sturdy hockey-playing sixth-former. Even more surprisingly David gave a graphic account of how he had followed a couple in the woods and watched their activities from a hidden vantage point.

Josh tried to join in, and soon began to sound as emptily stupid as the others.

At lunchtime, when the dinghy had sailed well beyond Henley, they ate sandwiches in a field and later chucked Paul in the river. He wasn't in the least put out, swimming around happily and then basking on the bank like a seal. When the others plunged in, however, he became a shark, swimming underwater, grabbing their legs and pulling them down into the dark green depths, from which they emerged spluttering, ducking each other and then making a concerted attempt to get Paul over and over again.

Eventually, they sailed on, easing the dinghy through another couple of locks until she bumped lazily against the bank. Exhausted by the horseplay and the open air, the five of them disembarked and stretched out in a field under the mellow sun.

Chapter Seven

JOSH WOKE to the buzzing of insects and tiny flutter-ings on his cheek. He glanced down at his watch to see that it was after six and realised he was being persecuted by swarms of little black flies now getting into his eyes and ears.

The others woke more slowly, but soon discovered that they were up against the same irritating problem.

"It's the poison swarm from hell," yelled Paul, beating wildly at the cloud of insects.

"There's only one thing for it," shouted Tom, for once taking over the leadership of the group. He ran down the slope and dived neatly off the bank, arching out into deeper water while the others followed, the black flies still in pursuit.

Josh sensed a change in the atmosphere, as if the hilarity was getting too much for all of them to bear. Rather than ducking and splashing each other, the boys swam around silently on their own, watching the black cloud on the bank with foreboding.

"They're only flies," Josh shouted.

Suddenly the river was cold, and when he stood up in the shallows he felt an unpleasant mush beneath his feet. The sun went behind a cloud.

Later, the *Moorhen* sailed on, her now shivering crew silent, downcast, despite the fact that the black flies showed no sign of pursuing them, still hovering in their cloud, clearly territorial.

There were no jokes, no shouting, no picking on anybody, just the water slapping against the bows of the dinghy. Clouds had gathered round the late evening sun, turning the landscape a dull burnt-out shade that reminded Josh of a photographic negative, but as he stared at it uneasily the sun came out again, bathing them in a gentle warm light that was more comforting.

"Signs and symbols," said the voice of Mr Acton, his English teacher, in Josh's mind. "Primitive man was always looking for signs and symbols to give reassurance to his life as he crouched round his fire."

That's what we need, thought Josh. A fire and somewhere to camp for the night.

The sign for Hawkins' Farm Camp Site appeared as if on cue.

"We could moor up to that tree," said Josh.

Jack frowned but nevertheless steered the dinghy towards the bank. "It's too early to camp," he objected.

"Not too early for food," said Paul. "We could get a fire going and cook a fry-up."

"That's a great idea," said Tom, but he sounded as artificial as Dad had at breakfast.

At first the camping seemed to proceed smoothly and efficiently. The farmer was helpful and even said they could pitch at some distance from the official site, in a field near the river.

Maybe he thinks we're going to be noisy, thought Josh, and was sure he was right when he saw the caravans and couples with young children. The farmer also agreed that they could light a fire, using dead wood from a nearby copse.

They cooked bacon, eggs and sausages on the primus stove. The food tasted delicious in the open air, and afterwards Paul brought out the cider. But no one seemed to want to drink it. Not even Paul. Josh felt stiff and awkward in their company, eventually drifting off into a light sleep on the grass.

Josh woke suddenly to find the others bending over him, grinning, their faces caked in mud.

"What's up?" he muttered.

"We're the Mud Warriors," said Paul with a stupid but somehow menacing grin.

"Who?" Josh was forcibly reminded of the dream he had had about the twins coated in body paint, playing so dangerously with their coloured swords.

"You are to take the Initiation Test," said Paul. "Tonight you are to become a man."

"What test?" asked Josh suspiciously. He didn't much like the game they were playing.

"You must go to the Mud Monster. You must worship him."

Paul was standing over Josh now, his belly sagging over the belt of his shorts.

"The Mud Monster," chanted Tom, Jack and David.

The night was hot and clammy and Josh knew that he was a victim again, that the others couldn't bear to be alone with their thoughts. They wanted action. They wanted distraction. Jack looked powerful – as if he was intent on proving himself. But proving what?

"You have to worship the Mud Monster," said Paul.

"Push off!" said Josh scornfully, but he knew he was afraid of them.

Seizing his arms and legs, they carried him struggling through a small copse, his face brushed by rasping twigs, until they stood over a narrow tributary whose soft mud oozed yawningly up at him in the moonlight.

"You're not going to throw me in there," Josh gasped, more angry than afraid now.

"You have to worship the Mud Monster," whispered Paul.

"Worship," chanted the other three. "Worship the Mud Monster."

They were beginning to swing him over the ditch, strong hands grasping his limbs no matter how hard he thrashed and kicked.

"Now!" they yelled and suddenly released him.

Josh seemed to fall for a very long time before he eventually hit the mud.

The stuff smelt like a sewer, and the more he squirmed the more he sank for the mud was thick, and as he tried to find a foothold he went deeper. He made a panicky grab at the bank, but the thin dry grass came away in his hands.

The others laughed and chanted. "Worship," they chorused as Josh sank up to his thighs. "Worship the Mud Monster."

It was Jack who was the first to realise that the game had gone sour.

"For God's sake stop struggling," he shouted.

"I'm sinking," yelled Josh, the fear like a steam hammer pounding in his head. "Get me out."

"Worship," Paul was still chanting.

"Shut up!" said Jack, his voice shaking. "Just shut up and get Josh out."

He lay down on his stomach, and Tom grabbed his ankles. Paul, looking distraught now, watched helplessly with a terrified David.

"Reach out to me," shouted Jack.

"I can't," bellowed Josh. He was still unable to get any purchase, for the mud was like quicksand. Feverish panic swept him and he began to cry hysterically, "Help me! Please help me!"

"I'm trying to," said Jack. "You've got to reach out. Throw yourself towards me." He was authoritative now.

"I can't move!"

"*Try.*"

"I'll only sink deeper."

"Reach out!"

Josh pushed himself over as far as he could, but his outstretched fingers only brushed Jack's hand. I'm going to die, he thought. The mud will swallow me up.

The twins were working as one now. Jack arched himself over the ditch while Tom firmly gripped his ankles.

"Josh – grab my wrist."

He reached up and made tenuous contact.

"I'm going to pull, so hang on. You ready, Josh?"

"Yes," he said, piteously dependent.

"Let's go."

For some time they pulled, but Josh remained just as firmly stuck and the panic swept back, making him bellow with fear.

"Pull harder," he pleaded.

Jack's face was red with effort. "I'm trying, aren't I?"

"Pull harder!" roared Josh.

Jack tried again, but still nothing happened and Josh looked up into David's eyes, seeing the terror in them.

"Pull!"

Suddenly, like a cork from a bottle, Josh seemed to explode from the mud with a terrific squelching, oozing sound and Jack, his face twisted in pain, landed him on firm ground like a slithering, sliding fish.

Josh lay face down, his mouth opening and closing, gasping for air, his hands rooted in dry earth.

"You bloody idiots," he managed to gasp out at last.

"Yes," snapped Jack. "We certainly are." He gazed angrily at Paul. "It was your fault, you fat clown."

"It was wicked," said David, his voice breaking. It was a strange choice of word, thought Josh even as he struggled for breath, the others standing stock still, staring at David, their eyes expressionless in the moonlight.

Josh rose stiffly to his knees; he was caked in the quickly drying mud.

"It's the Curse of the Mummy's Tomb," said Paul with laboured humour, knowing he couldn't turn it back into a joke but trying all the same.

"Shut up," said David with uncharacteristic belligerence, "or I'll chuck you in there myself."

"You and whose army?"

"Can't you see what you did – what you could have done?" David sounded utterly contemptuous, confident that the others were with him.

Paul gazed down at Josh contritely. "Sorry," he said.

"You're an idiot, Paul. What are you?" contributed Jack.

"An idiot," admitted Paul miserably.

"Except that we were all idiots," said David. "More than idiots."

Jack intervened abruptly. "Why don't you dive in the river, Josh? Get cleaned up?" He made it sound like another of his orders.

"It's too cold," muttered Josh.

"It's the only way you'll get all that mud off," pointed out Tom.

Josh knew he was right and shuffled to his feet.

"We'll put some hot soup on," said Jack. "I'll light the primus again." He sounded like Mum now – or how Mum used to sound. Comforting.

Josh dived. The water *was* cold, but it felt deeply refreshing as he ducked his head under the surface and struck out, not able to see anything except the occasional dark frond of weed. Even when his feet touched the shifting river bed and he felt the mulch at the bottom, he didn't mind. His fear had left him.

Josh surfaced gasping, and swam strongly to the bank and the four small figures standing round the primus stove, heads bowed, waiting for him.

Chapter Eight

As Josh scrambled out of the river he saw that most of the mud had washed off. Jack brought a towel and rubbed his brother's back gently, as he used to do when he took a much younger Josh to the swimming pool years ago. Jack had taught him to swim in the big echoing pool, and Josh could almost smell the chlorine now. Jack had been patient as he spluttered his way across the width. Eventually Josh had succeeded. He'd never forget Jack's face when he'd actually swum the width without putting his foot down. It had been full of pride and excitement. Then he had towelled him dry just as he was doing now. Except that tonight Jack's face was blank and his eyes were dead.

"That's all the mud off then," said Jack, while the other three looked on cautiously. "You OK?"

"Sort of." Josh wasn't going to let any of them off lightly.

"It was just a joke that went wrong," Tom assured him.

"Sure."

"Is that soup ready yet?" said Jack sharply.

Paul shambled off to check while Josh put on the change of clothes Mum had insisted they bring with them.

The oxtail soup was piping hot.

"Is it all right?" asked Tom solicitously.

Josh sipped and pronounced it satisfactory. "Did you put a hot-water bottle in my sleeping bag?" he asked him jokingly, but Tom took his question seriously.

"Go and fix it," he told Paul threateningly.

Unused to being the victim, Paul was almost tearful. "We haven't got one, have we?" He gazed wildly in the direction of the tents as if the hot-water bottle had been hidden there deliberately and his task was to discover its whereabouts.

"It was a joke," said Josh. "Just a joke." He shivered. "I'm going to turn in."

"Do you feel all right?" demanded Jack anxiously. "You're not hurt or anything?"

"No."

"I'll come and check you out in a minute."

"Kiss me goodnight?" Josh tried to inject some humour into the heavy atmosphere.

"No," grinned Jack, looking away. "I was going to leave that to Paul."

"Give him a smacker," advised David.

"Right on his arse," suggested Tom.

50

But Paul couldn't take any more teasing. "Leave it out," he snarled.

"Temper, temper," muttered David derisively.

Paul made a stumbling run at his brother, lashing out with his fists, but David was too quick for him, running off into the darkness with a laugh. Paul tried to go after him, but Tom and Jack grabbed his arms and held him firmly.

Slowly he subsided, breathing heavily.

Suddenly Josh couldn't take any more. Grabbing his mug of soup, he hurried over to the tent that he was to share with his brothers.

Tom followed him, waiting until Josh had snuggled down into his sleeping bag. "I want to ask you something, but I don't suppose this is a very good time." Tom was hesitant.

"Ask away." Josh tried to sound casual, wondering if his suffering had not been in vain. Was Tom going to confide in him at last?

"Do you think Mum and Dad are all right?"

"What do you mean?" Josh asked blankly. Were they in on the secret too? Everyone but him?

"It's just that I don't think they've been getting on that well recently."

"They'll come through," said Josh, knowing how banal he must sound. He was deeply disappointed that Tom obviously wasn't going to share anything with him after all. Maybe he was even trying to put up a smoke screen.

"You think so?" Tom seemed to be hanging on to his words and for once he wasn't detached.

"Yes," he said. "It's just a sticky patch, that's all." The cliché resounded mockingly in his ears.

"OK. See you in the morning then."

"See you."

Josh drew his sleeping bag up and tried to sleep. Once again Tom's words beat a grim tattoo in his mind. "We've got to tell someone. We can't just leave him there." Relentlessly the litany continued until Josh fell into a light doze and dreamt that he and Jack were sitting together in the dinghy under the trees, gazing down at dark water.

"Tell me the secret," he asked his brother, but Jack only grinned wolfishly and pointed at Mrs Laidlaw as she rose up from her watery grave.

Josh woke and glanced muzzily around the tent, at first not remembering where he was and then recalling the events of the evening with a creeping disquiet. He listened for the sleeping sounds of the twins but could hear nothing. Groping for his torch, he switched it on, only to find he was alone.

He looked at his watch. Just after three-thirty. Where were they? What could they be up to now? He scrambled out of his sleeping bag and checked the other two. They were still warm, so his brothers had not been gone long.

The tabs on the tent had been hastily tied together,

but when Josh pulled at them they gave way at once and he crawled out to find the parched grass moist with dew.

Then he saw them.

He kept well down in the long grass. Clouds shifted restlessly across the face of the moon, giving him shadowy cover as he stalked the older boys.

The four of them were standing under a willow tree at the head of the muddy inlet. Were they going to throw Paul in now? Were they holding some kind of kangaroo court?

Seeking the cover of a small but thick-trunked elder tree, Josh finally got near enough to overhear what they were saying.

"It's wicked," David was whispering.

"It happened." Jack sounded exhausted and his voice held little authority. "We can't make it unhappen, so we have to leave it alone."

"It's the only way." Paul, obviously no longer the victim, was much more assured. "There's nothing you should do, Dave." He spoke in a slightly wheedling tone. "Just leave it alone. You'll feel better soon."

"I won't," replied David bleakly.

"Listen." Tom's voice was as weary as Jack's but sounded frightened too. "There's nothing you can do."

"Of course there is. You *know* what we should *all* do," said David emphatically.

"You're out of your mind," said Jack. The authority was back but so was his anger, his voice rising.

"No," replied David shakily. "It's you – you're the one who's not thinking straight."

"Wait," Tom interrupted them. "You're talking too loudly – you'll wake Josh."

"There's nothing more to be said." David shrugged.

He began to walk back towards the tents, but Jack was on him before he had taken more than a couple of steps, wheeling him round.

"You start grassing us up and I'll fix you. Besides" – he paused and his voice grew a little softer – "you'll end up in the same trouble as the rest of us. What's your dad going to think?"

"Yes," said Paul glibly. "You can't hurt Dad. Not just like that."

Tom spoke reasonably, persuasively. "We've got to stand by each other, Dave. We can't afford not to. We've all got a conscience. Get it? You're not the only one. And you know what we have to do? Nothing. It's all too late now anyway. Try to forget it ever happened."

David stood before them, his chest heaving, as if he was facing a tribunal.

They all stopped talking. In the silence the gentle lapping of the river sounded menacingly loud.

"Got it?" asked Tom.

Reluctantly, David nodded.

His mind reeling, Josh crept away. As he crawled into the tent he could hear the sound of sobbing and then Jack's voice sharply rapping out, "Shut up. Josh is going to hear."

I've heard all right, he thought, but not enough. What have they done, he wondered as he buried himself deep into the warmth of his bag. What have they done?

When the twins returned, creeping noiselessly into the tent, Josh feigned sleep and hoped he was being convincing. In fact he was almost as terrified of them finding him awake as he had been of being sucked down by the mud. Jack and Tom were no longer his twin brothers, they were not even boys any longer; they were men.

Chapter Nine

JOSH WOKE sobbing. Jack was leaning over him, smelling of sweat. A grey darkness filled the tent.

"What the hell's the matter?"

Josh continued to sob until his brother shook him, gazing down at him anxiously.

"Bad dream," he muttered.

"Come and talk outside," said Jack. His voice was expressionless.

"What's going on?" murmured Tom sleepily.

"It's OK. Josh was having a dream. Come on."

Jack was out of his sleeping bag, standing in grubby shorts, the muscles in his arms taut.

The sky was a leaden grey with a pale dawn just beginning to show on the eastern horizon, the river a sullen blanket, shards of mist rising from its surface, on which the shadowy form of a swan glided.

"What were you dreaming about then?" Jack asked softly.

They had walked down to the water's edge, the ground damp beneath their bare feet.

"I don't know now." Josh felt paralysed by his brother's presence. Had Jack seen him watching?

"Come on—"

"It was a nightmare."

"Yes?"

"A horrible nightmare." Josh didn't know what to say. With the old Jack he would have come clean at once, but he was terrified of the new one.

"Is that all?"

There was nothing exactly threatening in Jack's voice, just a kind of dull probing, like a blunt needle.

"No." Josh suddenly decided to take the ultimate risk, more of an instinct than any kind of reasoned thought.

"Then what?' Jack's voice hardened, but there was apprehension in it too.

"Why was David so scared?" As Josh blurted out the question at last, he felt an overpowering sense of relief, but it was quickly replaced by foreboding.

Jack flinched and said nothing, his face expressionless.

"Why?" Josh repeated, all his bravado slipping away.

Still his brother didn't reply, but his face was working slightly and a vein beat in his temple. "Oh that," he said at last, trying to sound casual but completely failing.

"It was worse than the fight."

"Yes," said Jack. "Yes, it was worse."

Josh was the interrogator now.

"I'd better tell you," said Jack with sudden decision. "But you're not to—"

"I won't tell anyone." Josh knew he had to keep his brother's trust somehow. At last he had had the courage to confront him and he didn't want to blow it away now.

"You'd better not." There was menace in Jack's voice, but it was dwarfed by the eagerness with which he spoke, a determination to convince. "David did something really stupid. You know Gerry Tate?"

"He's in hospital. Didn't he fall off his bike?" Josh was trying to cope with his brother's sudden energy.

"David fixed his brakes."

Josh was silent, trying to analyse the information, hoping for more.

Eventually, after a long pause, Jack continued. "He shouldn't have done it. Gerry could have been killed."

"He's getting better though," said Josh hesitantly. Was this all? Was this the secret? It was like when Tom had spoken to him about their parents last night. Unsatisfactory. More than that.

"It's lucky that he is."

Another silence developed, during which Josh tried to say nothing in the hope that Jack would say more. But the waiting game was too much for him. "Why did David do it then?" he asked weakly.

"Gerry was bullying him. Beating him up."

"Why?" Josh persisted.

"You know what Dave's like."

He didn't exactly, but he let it go. "*You* were threatening to beat Dave up," he pointed out.

"I lost my temper."

"Like you did with Tom?"

"Sort of."

"I still don't understand."

"I haven't finished." Jack seemed more irritable than menacing now and Josh waited patiently. "David wanted to own up. We didn't think that was a good idea."

"Who's we?"

"Paul and Tom and me."

"But if he wanted to tell—"

"We'd have been in trouble too."

"Did you all fix Gerry's brakes then?" There was something very unconvincing about what Jack was saying, but Josh couldn't immediately work out what it was. His mind raced but failed to engage.

"No. But we knew Dave did it. He told us."

"I see." In fact Josh was now sure that he didn't.

"He kept it to himself in the end, but Tom thought he should tell too."

"That's why you had the fight?"

He nodded.

"But why did you threaten Dave like that?"

"I told you. I lost my temper. There's no point in him telling now. It's too late." Jack was speaking fast, his words tumbling over each other. "Gerry's a bully.

You know that. Well, he won't be bullying again." He sounded uncertain.

"He'll be lucky if he can ride again," said Josh bleakly.

"It's a kind of justice." Jack was looking at a point somewhere over Josh's shoulder.

"*Is* David going to own up?"

"Not now."

"You mean you've scared him?"

"I mean, he decided."

"Of his own free will?"

"Sure."

Once again, Josh had the impression he was talking to a stranger. This wasn't his brother. The brother he loved. It was someone else. Someone who was lying. The much delayed confrontation hadn't worked after all.

"So it's over."

"I hope so."

"But you threatened him. It wasn't of his own free will. You *made* him not tell." Josh was trying to reach Jack, still needing to extract the real truth.

"I know. I told you I lost my temper. It was bad and I've said I'm sorry."

"What does Tom think?"

"He's changed his mind. He thinks David should keep quiet."

"And Paul?"

"He always thought he should."

"You sure David isn't just scared of you?"

"He was, but now he's thought out the situation for himself . . . " Jack paused again. "Look, I know I haven't been myself recently – all this worry over David – but I've been rotten to you."

"It doesn't matter," said Josh guardedly, wondering how much more pressure he could put on.

"It *does*. So I'm going to treat you better. Get back to how we used to be. Right? Then you won't need to spy on me, will you?"

The threat was back.

Josh said nothing and Jack glanced at him warily, anxiety returning. "What do you think then?"

"About Gerry? I don't know."

"Do *you* think he should have owned up?" Jack persisted, and Josh had the feeling that his brother was trying to draw him in, manipulate his emotions, trade on his weakness.

"Not now," Josh replied uneasily.

"You're right," said Jack, patting his brother's shoulder reassuringly. "You're absolutely right. Now let's turn in."

He's won, thought Josh miserably. "I'll sit out here for a while," he said, despising himself. "I want to watch the dawn come up."

Jack looked at him suspiciously. "You don't believe me?"

"Of course I do." Was it that obvious, Josh wondered. But why didn't he come clean? Some-

61

thing was stopping him. Was he still afraid? Did he want to protect Jack? Make his brother dependent on him?

"I wouldn't like anything to come between us." There was a hint of the old threat in Jack's voice.

"Nothing could," said Josh numbly.

"OK." He seemed a little more satisfied. "I'm going back for a bit more kip. Don't get cold."

Josh knew he had to think. Desperately he tried to recall the conversation he had overheard earlier and fragments gradually returned to him.

"It's wicked."

Jack had winced and then frowned.

"It happened. We can't make it unhappen."

"It's the only way. You'll feel better soon."

"I won't."

"There's nothing you can do."

"You *know* what we should *all* do."

"You're out of your mind."

"No. It's you."

"You start grassing us up and I'll fix you," Jack had said. "You'll end up in the same trouble as the rest of us."

"We've got to stand by each other. We can't afford not to."

Josh recalled Tom's words even more clearly and with greater impact. "We've all got a conscience. Get it? You're not the only one. And you know what we have to do? Nothing."

It *could* all apply to the sabotage of Gerry's bike, except that it must mean that David was only one of the saboteurs. If they *had* all been involved, then Jack was simply scaring David into keeping quiet.

He was seeing another side to the twins – their secret side – bullying, at odds with each other, their consciences hurting but not hard enough to make them do the decent thing. That's what Dad would have said: "Do the decent thing." Now it seemed all four of them were locked together in a conspiracy, with David as the weak link.

Suddenly, Josh wanted his parents, just like Tom had. They represented safety, sanctuary, a grown-up world of responsibility, of being "all right". But *their* problems meant he couldn't approach them now. He must stay in his brothers' world, a world in which cracks had opened up. He was treading a crumbling surface; to understand what was going on he would need to go deeper.

Chapter Ten

THE TENSION was increasing as they sailed home, and the weather had changed to suit Josh's mood. Storm clouds built up as the humidity rose, a frazzle of lightning forked the sky and there was the ominous growl of distant thunder.

For a while there was little wind – just a period of anticipation as the *Moorhen* tacked sluggishly, her sails hardly filling, the sky dark purple and swollen.

No one spoke much; Jack gave curt commands and Josh wondered just how long the journey was going to take. He wanted to get home, to adjust himself to what had happened – or what might have happened. Above all, he wanted to be on his own, to think, to plan what to do next.

The wind came in fitful gusts and then blew more strongly, until the *Moorhen* was scudding along on a fast reach. Jack ordered Tom and Paul out on the starboard bow with David and Josh sitting opposite.

Then Jack surprised him. "When we go about you two stay where you are and we'll have Josh and Dave out on the bow." Josh felt a rush of pleasure at Jack's recognition, and he scrambled up to obey him. Despite all that had happened, the ferocious tacking of the dinghy was sheer delight: the *Moorhen*'s prow so cleanly cleaving the dark water, the spray lashing their faces, the spars creaking with the sails full of the driving wind as they streaked across the Thames.

Every time they went about, David and Josh ducked under the boom, trampled past Tom and Paul and threw themselves to the other side, grabbing the sheets and leaning out as far as they could to keep the dinghy stable.

Jack winked at him. "Brilliant, isn't it?"

"Fantastic," Josh replied, but he was afraid of that wink. Suddenly it was all part of the conspiracy.

The rain came, slowly at first, pitting the surface with tiny darts until a torrential downpour dispersed the wind and the dinghy was becalmed. Within seconds all five were completely soaked, the shore disappearing into a thickening mist.

"Wish we had an outboard," said Paul, shaking with the sudden chill.

"We haven't," snapped Tom unfeelingly. "You'll have to get bailing. And don't tell me there isn't a bucket."

"There isn't a bucket," said David dismally.

Gradually the force of the rain lessened, until only spitting drops hit the surface. The mist slowly cleared and the sun began to break through the grey clouds with fleeting warmth. As its rays grew fiercer their clothes began to steam, but there was no wind and they were still becalmed.

"We'll have to row," said Tom.

Jack gave the wolfish grin Josh had dreamt about. "Good idea. Tom and Josh, you're the galley slaves. I'll stay at the helm."

"Are you ever anywhere else?" muttered Paul mutinously.

Rowing home seemed to take hours. By the time a small breeze blew up they were exhausted; even Jack looked drained, his eyes closing, hand rigidly clutching the tiller, hardly noticing where he was steering. Several times they swung towards the bank and he only just corrected the *Moorhen*'s course at the last moment.

"Let me take over," urged Tom. "You're shattered."

"I'm the only one who knows what he's doing," came the sullen reply.

"You sure?" asked Paul, grimacing.

"Shut up." Jack tried to concentrate, to reassert his authority.

When the *Moorhen* arrived back at Henley, Josh felt an overwhelming sense of relief. It was as if they had been away for months.

Once past the town the breeze freshened and plucked at the sails and the dinghy's course was less erratic.

She was on the final reach when David said, "I think I'm going to be sick."

"Not here you're not," yelled Paul.

But Jack was more practical. "Stick your head over the side. Not that one, you idiot. The wind will blow it back all over you."

"And us," said Tom mournfully.

David managed to get his head in the right position and was sick for a very long time, until all he could retch up was a thin bile.

"I'll never get him home on that bike," Paul complained.

"I'd run him back if only we had the . . ." Jack paused, gazing at them fearfully, and the other three stared back at him in horrified silence ". . . if only Dad or Mum would let me drive the car." Jack's face reddened in confusion. Paul looked angry now, and Tom concerned. What was the matter, wondered Josh. What had he said? Jack had always been fascinated by cars and had been pestering Dad for months for an old banger to practise on in the field behind the house. But why had the others looked at him like that? As if Jack had given something away.

Once they had returned to dry land, Josh, Paul and Tom unloaded the dinghy, while David and Jack strolled over to the Tyler house to fetch the key of the boat shed.

Josh helped to drag out the sodden tents, spreading them on the lawn to dry, followed by the damp clothes, rucksacks, dirty plates, pots and pans and the remains of the food. Josh, Tom and Paul worked silently, obviously wanting to get away from each other. Josh felt they had all been together for far too long now and he knew – or thought he knew – every little mannerism or irritating trick of speech of each of his companions.

Jack and David didn't return and the implications of their departure suddenly broke into Josh's fatigue. At once he knew he had to locate his brother, find out what was going on. Had he taken David away to give him another warning?

"I must have a pee," he said, unable to think of a better excuse.

"Go in the river then," said Paul through a yawn.

"That's pollution," he replied quickly.

"Go in the house and be quick about it." Tom ran his hands through his dirty hair as if in despair.

Josh was sure that David and Jack would be in the shrubbery where the fight had taken place. That was the most private part of the garden, the most likely place for them to go.

He padded across the lawn, then slowed down and listened. Sure enough he could just pick out the hushed urgency of voices, but he had to get closer to find out whether or not what they were saying would corroborate Jack's story.

As he moved cautiously towards the thick laurel bushes, he realised that this would be the third time he had eavesdropped on his brother. He'd become a spy, not trusting anyone, determined to find out the truth for himself.

At last he was near enough to hear what they were saying, pressing himself up against the foliage, listening to Jack's voice, soft but full of menace.

"So you understand *now*?"

"Yes." David's voice was practically inaudible and Josh was sure that he had been crying.

"Josh is suspicious."

"I didn't tell him anything."

"You don't have to. It's the way you look."

"I can't help that."

"You have to." Jack sounded as if he was at the end of his patience. "You know what'll happen if you don't."

"I wish I was dead," said David with such heartfelt conviction that Josh shivered.

"You will be if you go down there again."

"I just had to."

"But why?"

"I felt like someone should be with him."

"Don't be such a fool." Jack's anger was mounting. "Listen to me, David. I'm going to say this for the last time. If you go down to the pit I'll – I'll kill you."

Josh felt as if a cold hand was squeezing his heart. He had never heard such a lethal tone to Jack's voice before. It was terrifying and Josh felt numb, unable to move, ready to be confronted by his brother. Secret Jack. Murderous Jack.

But what did he mean by the pit? Was that where they had sabotaged Gerry's bike? It just didn't add up. There had to be more to this than the sabotaging of a bike, however destructive the results. Josh racked his brains for an explanation but couldn't find one. Once again he saw the horrified look in their eyes when Jack had mentioned the car. What car?

He listened to the silence between David and Jack, then heard them move over the long grass towards him, their footsteps soft and barely discernible.

Thinking that they were nearer than they were, a tide of panic swept over him, and as before Josh found himself unable to move. Then, in sudden desperation, he conquered his paralysis and ran as lightly and as fast as he could back towards the house, hurtling round the corner, coming to a panting halt at the back door. It was locked.

Without thinking, he rattled at the handle until he remembered the key was under a stone. He bent down and tugged it out and shakily inserted it into the lock. The old rusty key seemed wilfully stiff, refusing to turn as, whimpering with fear, he twisted it this way and that.

If Jack and David came round the corner now he would be done for. They would both leap to the conclusion that he had been spying on them and they would be dead right. Dead. He shuddered again as he twisted the key. Was Jack capable of killing someone?

Suddenly the door swung open and Josh almost

threw himself inside, leaving it ajar and running towards the toilet. He had to establish his alibi fast. Once inside, he sat down on the seat gasping. "If you go down to the pit I'll kill you." The words clamoured in Josh's mind until the pain in his head became excruciating.

Chapter Eleven

FIVE MINUTES later Josh flushed the toilet and emerged, just as the front door closed quietly. "Who's there?" he asked guiltily.

"Jack," came the monotone reply.

Josh's heart pounded as he saw his brother standing in the hall, his dark hair and brown face swathed in a halo of sunlight. His arm muscles bulged, and despite his dirty T-shirt and shorts he looked like a vengeful warrior, come to claim his victim.

"Where have you been?" Jack asked. His grey eyes were steel, his arms were folded.

"Having a pee."

"Is that all?"

"Sure."

"You haven't been spying on me again?"

"No."

Jack came closer, his hands by his sides now, a thin smile on his lips, challenging him.

"I think you might have been doing just that."

"I went for a pee," Josh replied defensively.

"Did you now?"

"Why *should* I spy on you? You've told me what happened." Josh tried to control himself. "Is David still being..."

Jack was very close now, assessing him, searching for flaws. "He'll be all right."

"OK."

"You believed what I said, didn't you, Josh? When we had that chat this morning."

"Yes," replied Josh woodenly.

"Got any more questions?"

"No."

"You look as if you're full of them."

"Well, I'm not."

Josh wondered how much his brother suspected. Had he really given himself away so completely?

"OK." Jack suddenly relaxed. "You look dead tired."

That word again, thought Josh.

"How was the trip?" Mum asked as she opened tins in the kitchen while Josh sat at the table, wishing he didn't have to talk, trying to think of an excuse to go up to his room.

"Great."

"Wet, wasn't it?"

"Slightly."

"Dinghy go well?"

"Like a bomb."

All the time she was asking him questions, Josh was thinking about the pit. What pit? An actual pit? He had never heard of one, not round here anyway.

"You caught that terrible storm."

"It was exciting," replied Josh vaguely.

Maybe it wasn't an *actual* pit. Could it have another meaning? Be a code word for something?

"And everyone got on all right?"

Josh remembered David's misery. "Like a house on fire," he said dutifully, aware of the irony in the cliché.

"Jack's a bit off colour, isn't he?"

"What do you mean?" said Josh sharply, surprised she had stepped on to the dangerous ground that she had previously tried to ignore. Does she know something, he wondered yet again. What's her game? Is that what they were all really doing? Playing games?

"He's not himself," she said obliquely and then came closer to the point. "Nervy and washed out," she added hesitantly.

"We didn't get much sleep."

"It's more than that, isn't it?"

It certainly was, but what had she spotted? Josh was very tense now.

"I always wish . . . " She sighed and paused in mid-sentence, emptying baked beans into a saucepan. "But there it is."

"What are you on about, Mum?" asked Josh impatiently.

"I know how Jack worships his father. If only Dad

would do more with him, reach out a bit." She clattered all the empty tins into the refuse bin.

"He's always busy. Like you."

She deliberately ignored the accusation.

"I just wish they could go sailing together."

"Like we used to go to Temple Island?"

For the first time she looked straight at him.

"We must take an expedition out there soon," she said quickly, making it sound like a trip across the Atlantic.

"When you're not so busy," muttered Josh. "Jack was close to me – he's never been that close to Dad."

He felt competitive, and Mum shook her head as if she couldn't cope with it all. But how much did she want to, he wondered.

That night Josh slept deeply, but towards morning he drifted into shallower sleep and dreamt of the pit, a hole in the ground that was dark and dry and dusty. He was standing inside it, looking up the shaft. Someone had once told him that if you stood at the bottom of a well, and it was deep enough, you could see the stars in the sky in broad daylight. Now, in his dream, Josh could see them twinkling behind a bright blue morning, with the sun a burning red orb.

The twins were up at the top of the pit, peering down at him, and were soon joined by Paul and David. Paul was in a clown's costume, but the other three were in T-shirts and shorts.

"Riddle me ree," began Paul. "Can't tell a boy from a tree. Riddle me ro. In the pit you must go."

Jack leant over the edge and said, "If you go down to the pit, I'll kill you."

David joined him. "I only want to be with you," he explained. "That's all."

"You can't get me!" yelled Josh. "I'm down here – you're up there. It's too steep to climb down." He didn't add that the sides were also too steep to climb up.

"Can't I?" Jack started making a buzzing sound, and as he rose above the pit Josh could see that the lower half of his brother's body had become that of a wasp.

Jack buzzed down the shaft, the huge sting in his tail blotting out the sun.

Josh struggled awake, trying to drive the Jack wasp away. Grey light filled the room and he knew it was early, just like the previous morning, down by the river. Was he always going to wake up at dawn, exhausted by nightmares?

He got up, knowing he wouldn't be able to sleep any longer, pulled one curtain open and gazed down at the river. There was very little mist this morning and Josh knew the day was going to be hot. The surface of the water had a slight haze and the sky was already turning a pale blue.

Then he saw Jack and Tom pushing their bikes

slowly and furtively from the shed. He quickly closed the curtain, knowing they would soon look up at the house to make sure they hadn't been spotted.

When Josh cautiously peered out again, he saw the twins cycling up the towpath towards Henley.

Chapter Twelve

JOSH DRESSED hurriedly. The long straight towpath had very little cover and at this time of the morning there would be hardly anyone around. The twins would have every chance of seeing him, yet Josh still felt compelled to go after them. He couldn't let the opportunity slip. He had to discover the whereabouts of this pit. Maybe they were going there now.

Josh crept down the stairs, opened the back door and hurried to the shed. He pulled his bike out and then quickly pedalled through the garden, over the green sward by the river and up the towpath. The air smelt clean and rain-washed and despite his fears Josh felt a sense of purpose burning inside him. He was sure he was getting somewhere at last.

The twins must have been cycling fast, Josh thought, for they had covered a considerable distance. He could see clearly for hundreds of yards and there was absolutely no sign of them anywhere. A truck moved slowly over Henley Bridge and a baby was crying in a moored cruiser, but the riverside was almost deserted as Josh cycled on, past the rowing club and up towards the town.

Then he heard the low whistle just behind him.

He stopped and turned round. He couldn't see anyone, but he thought the whistle might have come from the grounds of the rowing club, which was set back from the river. He hesitated, feeling completely exposed and not knowing what to do. Then the whistle came again.

He turned his bike round and slowly cycled into the grounds. Nearing the club, he was suddenly conscious of movement behind him. He stopped again, dismounted and turned back towards the boathouse. One of its doors was opening.

As they cycled towards him the twins were grinning, but not unpleasantly, and for a moment Josh wondered if they were going to be friendly.

"Fancy seeing you," said Tom.

"You don't give up, do you?" Jack's grin seemed to stretch from ear to ear. It was rigid, as if cast in cement, never leaving his face as he lazily rode over. Closer to, Josh could see that Jack's eyes were cold and blank.

He could have kicked himself; they had set a trap for him and his curiosity had driven him straight into it.

"You don't give up," repeated Jack. "Do you?"

"I don't get you," said Josh defensively.

"I think you do."

"OK. I saw you riding out. I thought it might be fun to follow you."

"Fun?"

"Well—" Josh hesitated, knowing how badly he was doing.

"You were spying on us." Jack spat the words out.

"Just curious."

Jack turned to Tom. "He didn't believe me. I told him what the trouble was, but he doesn't trust me."

Tom said nothing, the old inward-looking expression on his face.

"I *did* believe you," protested Josh unconvincingly.

"Then why follow us?"

"I don't know," he replied doggedly.

"You don't *know*." Jack sounded like Dad.

"No!"

"How can I get through to you?" Jack got off his bike and laid it on the grass, advancing on him, one fist clenched. "You won't listen to reason."

"I *will*."

"You need something to remember."

Josh glanced at Tom. He was no longer laid-back but startled and apprehensive instead.

Josh flung down his own bike and waited, watching the clenched fist.

Then Jack turned away.

"Why were you going to punch me?" he asked.

Jack didn't reply.

"He's afraid. That's why," said Tom.

At last Tom had reacted. He looked shaken, as if violence had only narrowly been averted.

"You shut up," said Jack. "Now."

Josh hesitated, looking from one to the other. "Afraid of what? Why don't you tell me the truth?" he said at last, gazing up at Tom imploringly.

But Tom didn't reply and Josh realised he had missed – just missed, perhaps only by a fraction of a second – an important opportunity. Maybe Jack *should* have hit him. Then Tom would have given more away.

"You've got to stop following us around." Jack's voice shook slightly.

"Where were you going then?"

"Just for a ride."

"At this time of the morning?" Josh was determined not to back down.

"Why not?"

"After yesterday?"

Tom came to Jack's rescue. "We couldn't sleep, so we thought we'd take some exercise." The mask was back on.

"*Is* there anything else?" asked Josh obliquely.

"What do you mean?"

"Anything you haven't told me?"

"No. Of course there isn't."

Josh turned to Tom. "Is there?" he persisted.

There was a pause.

"Tom?" asked Josh.

"Of course there isn't. Why don't you shut up!" Jack was clenching his fists again.

"Why can't he answer for himself?"

"Whatever Jack told you is the truth," said Tom too quickly. "He's been under a lot of strain," he added.

"Do you know *what* he told me?" demanded Josh.

"That David had fixed Gerry's bike and we did a cover-up."

Josh felt slightly deflated as the twins regained solidarity. The crack had surfaced but Tom had papered over it.

"We'll go on with our ride then." Jack paused questioningly. Then he shrugged and the twins rode away.

Why hadn't he mentioned the pit? Why had he held back yet again? Josh didn't know the answers. He watched his brothers ride off down the towpath, then picked up his own bike and cycled home. What was it about his brothers' relationship? Were they now simply bonded together by fear?

The river glistened in the pale sunlight, the wash from a passing launch hitting the grassy banks with a gentle slapping sound. Josh wished he was on Temple Island; life always seemed much clearer there. He glanced at his watch. No good thinking about the island now; it was a few minutes before seven and his parents would be getting up.

Then he saw Trev.

He was making his way down the road, delivering newspapers as he did every day. Why hadn't Josh thought of him before? He might know about the pit.

Trev was dodgy and had been in some undisclosed trouble that the Tyler parents had shaken their heads over. "He's got a very deprived background," Mum had said. Although Trev wasn't a client of hers he was "known" to the social services and was often "in trouble with the law".

But so far sixteen-year-old Trev hadn't been sent down, and however "dodgy" his activities might be, this did not apply to his paper rounds which he conducted with maximum, almost obsessive, efficiency. Whatever the weather, Trev was never late. The papers were delivered, even in the snow.

"If only the world was a paper round," Dad had said. "It's his pride. Like a shoeshine boy."

Josh had never actually seen a shoeshine boy but he knew that his father was being patronising, just like he had been to Jack when he had such good results in a school exam. "Not bad," he had told him, "but you can still do much better."

Trev was tall and dark, with a cast in his eye that made him look as if he was staring at a point somewhere over the top of Josh's head.

"Simple operation could correct that," Mrs Tyler had explained. "But apparently his parents can't be bothered."

Sometimes Josh wondered what his parents would do if Trev wasn't around. Then they wouldn't have anyone to patronise or anything to agree about.

83

"Hi."

Josh had always got on with Trev because they shared a common interest in the comic strip anti-hero Judge Dredd.

"You're up early."

If only he knew why, thought Josh. "I want to ask you something."

"Haven't got time. Can't be late on the round." Trev wanted to cycle on. Too many people asked him questions and he never liked answering them.

"It's only about this pit."

"Pit?"

"Some boys were talking about a pit somewhere round here."

"Don't know of no pit."

"It's a large – sort of hole in the ground."

"I know what a pit is, stupid. You sending me up?"

"No," said Josh hurriedly. "I just want to know where it is."

"Why?" said Trev suspiciously.

"I said I'd meet a mate there."

"Bad luck then. I don't know where it is."

"Please, Trev."

"Haven't a clue."

"I'll buy you a *2000 AD*."

"I can buy me own."

They were at an impasse.

Then Trev seemed to soften slightly. "Wait a minute," he said grudgingly. "Maybe they mean the old

84

quarry down Beverley Lane – just before the road branches off to Troughton. That's steep-sided enough. They say it was the devil's pit one time."

"Which time?"

"Long time ago. Anyway, there's just a lot of old car wrecks down there. Scrap dealer rented the place to do a bit of breaking in."

"Breaking in?"

Trev shot him a scornful look. "You pratt."

"Why am I a pratt?"

"Not breaking in – not into a house like. Bloke's breaking up cars. Smashing them. Get it?"

Josh nodded, feeling foolish.

"Got to be going now." Trev was impatient and rather scornful.

"Thanks a lot."

"What about *2000 AD* then?" He sounded truculent now.

"You said you didn't want it."

"Changed me mind, didn't I?"

"Take mine. It's due today."

Trev hesitated. "It's marked out to you."

"So what? Just take it."

"You sure?"

"Yes."

"I've got to deliver it." He was suddenly bureaucratic.

"All right. Give me the papers then." Josh sighed. Why was life so complicated? Trev handed them over and Josh took out the comic and passed it back to him. "Satisfied?" he asked.

Trev nodded, stuck the comic in his back pocket and cycled on without looking back.

"So you're the newspaper boy today?" asked Dad, who was writing a letter at the desk in the living room. He was even more jovial this morning and because of this Josh suspected he'd just had a row with Mum. She was sitting in the kitchen and the atmosphere was chilly. "Twins still in bed?" he asked.

"They went out for a bike ride," said Josh, realising his brothers' absence hadn't been noticed. He was now sure his parents *had* been arguing, for Mum always tapped on their bedroom doors in the morning and would come in if there was no answer.

"*This* early?" Her voice was subdued, distant.

"The early worm ..." Even Dad frowned, conscious he was overdoing the heartiness.

"I don't know what's got into those two." Mum emerged from the kitchen, looking eager, the way she always did after she had been crying.

Josh felt a nasty empty feeling in his stomach. What had been going on? Why didn't he just ask his parents, he wondered. Why hadn't he asked the twins about the pit? Why was it that he could never ask the important questions?

"They're all right," Dad was saying. "Up with the lark and—"

"For God's sake shut up," screamed Mum suddenly. "If I ever hear you say that again—"

"What have I done?" Dad was all injured innocence. "Just what did I say?"

"Not enough!" she said obscurely as she banged the kitchen door behind her.

"Your mother's not so well this morning," muttered Dad. "I think she's getting herself overtired. This conference has been so exhausting that—"

Josh didn't hear any more. He was thinking too hard.

Chapter Thirteen

HIS PARENTS stayed in Josh's mind as he cycled down the lane that ran round the back of the house. People changed without warning. One moment Mum and Dad were getting on all right and the next they were like strangers to each other, just as Jack and Tom had so rapidly become to him. It all seemed to happen in a moment, and Josh couldn't trust anyone now. Nor could he even bring himself to question them, to come straight to the point. It was as if there was an invisible wall between them, but it had been created by himself. He wanted things to be back to normal all the time – when they weren't. He had to face the fact that his family was breaking up all round him.

After pedalling hard for a mile or so, Josh took a left-hand turn on to a dusty track that snaked away across abandoned countryside, ditches filled with old prams and paper sacks of garden waste and gullies dark with pools of water that had collected at the bottom of rough meadows. The rusting hulk of a car loomed monstrously from one such pool and a couple of old bikes lay tangled together in another, half in and half out of the brackish water. Trev had said the place was known as the devil's quarry and the idea beat in Josh's mind.

More evidence of the devastation appeared with increasing frequency as Josh cycled on down the track, and over all there hung a stench of mechanical decay, petrol and diesel oil mixed with wild garlic. Josh noticed that the dried mud of the track was now scored by the marks of cycle tyres. So people came here. But why?

A crow flew noisily overhead and he was startled by the barking of a fox. The rising heat sharpened the pungent smell, and when he passed the remains of a young rabbit killed by some predator Josh began to feel sick. Slowly the track dipped, the sun seared his back and the sky above him was an intense blue.

He plunged down into the valley, but there were stunted trees and foliage on either side of him and he couldn't see what lay below. Then, as the descent steepened, the undergrowth suddenly dropped away and there, at the bottom of a steep cliff, was the quarry.

The place was a startling sight, piled high with butchered vehicles, glinting metallically in the harsh sunlight, a tarnished mirror winking here, a battered hubcap flashing there. It was a mechanical graveyard, approached by a rough track and surrounded by sagging fencing. A small office behind a locked front

gate was dominated by a big sign proclaiming: HARRI-
SON'S AUTO SALVAGE.

Josh cycled on, the dust hazing above him, his thirst
increasing. He wished he was back at the river that
always made him feel alive, invigorated, rather than at
this stinking hole in the ground that gave him such an
acute sense of being shut in. Flies buzzed around his
head and he saw a wasp's nest in a dead oak tree.
Despite the oppressive heat, Josh shivered. He felt
something or someone was watching him.

Dismounting from his bike, he pushed it up to the
barbed wire and noticed a couple of old tractors among
the wrecks, but they, too, looked abandoned.

There was a padlock on the front gate with a hole
in the bulging wire beside it, but Josh wasn't tempted to
clamber through. Instead, he got back on his bike and
began to ride around the perimeter fence, narrowly
avoiding the encroaching undergrowth that was clearly
poised to take over the breakers' yard and was already
sending long vine-like claws over the wire.

Then Josh saw dust rising on the hill above him and
knew that other cyclists were on their way. Quickly
pushing the bike behind a bush, he hid himself in
among the rasping, rustling leaves of an overgrown
beech hedge. Who were these cyclists? If it was the
twins, what would Jack do if he found Josh? All he
could do was wait.

Chapter Fourteen

JOSH HAD never seen these two boys before. They were both about sixteen and had closely shaved heads.

Doubled up in the hedge, he watched as they dumped their bikes and clambered through the hole in the fence, disappearing somewhere among the long stacks of smashed vehicles. The two boys looked confident and had an air of excitement about them.

After what seemed to be a very long time, Josh heard the reluctant whirring of an engine not quite firing on all cylinders. Then it suddenly roared into life and an old Ford Cortina came into view, driving at speed along the track that ran round the inside of the fence.

The Cortina, minus a couple of windows and with a huge, rusty dent along its nearside door, increased its revs and hurtled past Josh, bodywork rattling, a hubcap falling and bouncing towards the fence, a thick cloud of dust rising.

Then the beaten-up old banger disappeared again,

leaving behind it a rich mixture of exhaust fumes. When it returned at even greater speed, the driver stamped on the brakes and the Cortina slewed across the track, bald tyres screaming, brushing an old delivery van with a whine of rasping metal and then speeding up again to vanish on the other side of the pit.

The old car skidded round the corner and braked fiercely, but this time didn't hit the van. For a moment it was stationary, ticking over noisily, and Josh seized his opportunity, forcing himself to break cover. He choked as he clambered through the hole in the fence and ran towards the dust cloud, just as the Cortina was about to start up again.

"Hang on!" he yelled.

The boy poked his head out of the broken window. "What the hell do *you* want?" He didn't sound friendly.

"I just wondered ..." Josh began hesitantly.

"Wondered what?"

"Whether this place is still open?" The question sounded incredibly stupid, particularly as the quarry was in such a terrible state of dereliction, but Josh had acted so impulsively that he couldn't think of anything else to say.

"Does it look like it?" The reply was reasonable enough, but there was also a gathering hostility.

Slowly, forbiddingly, the two boys got out of the old car and strolled across to him, looking like two stick men in the blinding sunlight, with their shaven heads and pale, suspicious, indoor faces.

"This dump closed down months ago."

"Yes." Josh strove for further questions and then came clean. "I was looking for my brothers. They're twins."

"What are you up to?" snapped the taller of the two skinheads. "Come to grass us up, have you?"

"No," Josh protested. More grassing now? There seemed to be no end to it. "I think my brothers *may* come down here, but they won't tell me. It's their secret."

The two skinheads seemed to relax slightly.

"So you'd like to scare yourself rigid, would you?"

Josh said nothing. He didn't want to antagonise them even more.

"Want to come for a drive?"

"No, thanks."

"Come on. It's great. If you do, I'll tell you about your brothers." He grinned maliciously. "But you've got to pass the test first."

"What test?" Josh asked warily.

"Get in. You're going for a ride."

Chapter Fifteen

JOSH SAT fearfully on the partly collapsed back seat. The inside of the car smelt musty and damp.

"The name's Shane," said the driver, sounding strangely polite.

"I'm Graham," said the other boy. "What's your name?"

"Josh," he replied miserably.

"Well, Josh, we'll take a spin." Shane's voice was mocking. "I'm likely to jump on the brakes a couple of times, so sit well back in your seat for safety and comfort. Sorry there aren't any seatbelts. Ready?"

Josh nodded grimly.

The engine whirred and rattled into noisy life, starting off with a jerk and beginning to build up speed, hot air blowing in through the broken windows.

Graham glanced over his shoulder and grinned as the car shrieked round a bend and the inside filled with the smell of burning rubber. Then they were on the straight for a while, but this only provided an opportunity for Shane to accelerate so he could skid round the corners. Shutting his eyes made Josh feel sick, so instead he watched the stacks of car wrecks blur alongside him as Shane gunned the accelerator, determined to scare Josh with his erratic driving.

Gradually, however, the speed, the skidding, the burning rubber, the increasing smell of petrol and the lurching to and fro became so relentless that Josh actually began to adapt to it. He knew that the Cortina could turn over any moment and possibly burst into flames, but he fought against that vision. He was determined not to give the skinheads the pleasure of seeing him afraid, and maybe, if he could keep his face expressionless, Shane would get bored and put a stop to the agony of it all.

Perversely, Shane seemed determined to increase the speed, to take more risks, to get some reaction out of Josh at any cost, and the worst moment came when the Cortina lurched over on two wheels while rounding a bend. The car clipped the shell of an old VW with a rending scream of metal, and for a second Josh was certain they were going to overturn, but somehow Shane steered the Cortina back on all four wheels again and they sped on.

After a while the engine mercifully began to cough and they slid to a slow, dusty halt.

"That's it then," said Shane.

"What is?" asked Josh, trying to sound as cool and as laid-back as possible. It wasn't easy.

"We're out of juice. And we couldn't afford to buy

any this morning. So that's the end of your ride."

"I think the kid did pretty well," said Graham unexpectedly.

"Yes," agreed Shane grudgingly. "At least he didn't wet himself. Or have you?"

"No," said Josh with some dignity. "Now are you going to tell me if my brothers come down here? I mean – I've passed the test, haven't I?"

Slowly Shane nodded. "What do they look like then?"

Josh described Jack and Tom in some detail and even took the risk of giving their names, but neither Shane nor Graham seemed to recognise them.

"We know most kids who come down here," Shane said. "But I don't remember them two."

Neither did Graham. "We have banger races," he volunteered.

"And demolition derbies," contributed Shane.

"Do many of the cars work?" asked Josh.

"Some. You got to understand mechanics to get 'em started like." Shane was enthusiastic now. "You got to know your stuff."

"Don't any adults ever come down here?"

"You bet your life they don't." He paused. "Well, there was this old geezer we saw a couple of times, but he don't come here no more."

"I won't tell anyone," promised Josh.

"You'd better not," came the sour reply.

"You're welcome to come for a drive any time,"

grinned Graham challengingly, "or even get behind the wheel."

"Thanks," said Josh uneasily.

He rode back up the littered hillside, glad to get away from the quarry, hoping the twins had not been there. Jack would love to drive one of the old bangers, so Josh wasn't going to say anything about the place. Then he remembered something. "I'd run him back if only we had the – if only Mum or Dad would let me drive the car." The horrified looks, the change of tack, the tension, as if another little bit of the granite round the secret had been chipped away. Jack driving cars? Here? "We've got to tell someone. We can't leave him there," said Tom's voice in his mind.

His thoughts confused, Josh rode down the other side of the hill, relieved to be heading for the river.

It was almost midday and the sunlight gave the water a silver sheen. An eight furrowed its gleaming surface, while their coach cycled along the bank, bellowing instructions through a megaphone.

Nearing home, Josh saw another cyclist on the towpath, and as he approached he realised it was David, head down, his long hair flying behind him, wobbling about, hardly looking where he was going.

As he approached, Josh yelled, "Watch out!"

David came to a shuddering halt, and when he looked up his eyes were brimming with tears.

"What's the matter?" Josh demanded.

"Nothing."

"Come on. What is it?"

"I'm fine."

"You cry when you're fine?" He was determined to crack down, to be far more probing. "Has Jack been bullying you again?"

"No."

"Then why are you crying?"

"I fell off my bike."

"Were you hurt?"

"It was just – just the shock."

They gazed into each other's eyes.

"You're lying," Josh said firmly.

"Thanks!"

"I mean it."

"It's none of your business what I'm doing, so just get out of my way." David's voice wobbled, only making Josh even more determined not to be fobbed off.

"Tell me what's going on."

"Nothing."

"Liar!" Josh was determined to keep the pressure up. "Listen, Dave, tell me. *Please* tell me what's going on."

"I've got nothing to tell you and there's nothing going on." David ran his hand through his hair, flicking a lock away from his eye. "Now get out of the way!"

"Dave seemed upset," said Josh as he got off his bike.

"Did he?" Jack and Tom were coming out of the house with the cricket gear. "Want a game?" They were both elaborately casual.

"It's lunchtime."

"We thought we'd have a knock-up."

"OK."

Josh wanted to stay close to the twins. He was sure that it was the only way the situation could be brought to a head.

"But what's up with him then?" he persisted.

"I don't know." Jack shrugged. "Still worrying about you know what." Josh caught a look of sudden alarm flicker across Tom's face. "He'll be OK," continued Jack smoothly. "It just takes time."

"For what?"

"For him to stop feeling bad."

They put up the stumps and played a desultory game in the hot sun, but Jack didn't have his mind on cricket at all. He even allowed Josh to bat and Tom bowled gently, actually encouraging him to hit the ball. Eventually he did, and as it rose in the air Jack ran for the catch, but his concentration was poor and he dropped it, hardly bothering to be angry with himself.

Later, when Josh bowled consistent wides at Tom, there were no recriminations, and Jack patiently fielded without comment.

After a while it became obvious that the knock-up was a total non-event, and without saying anything, as if admitting defeat, the twins waited until Josh had finished bowling, pulled up the stumps and then walked back to the house as if he no longer existed.

"Thanks for the game," he called after them.

They nodded vaguely, too preoccupied to reply.

Josh watched them go in, not in the least hungry for his corned-beef sandwiches. Instead he wandered down to Temple Island, slipped off his T-shirt and, diving into the river, swam across in his shorts. Again the silky water soothed him, and as he clambered up the overgrown bank he felt a fleeting sense of peace.

Chapter Sixteen

JOSH SAT on the cracked steps, the flaking columns behind him, a bee buzzing among some foxgloves and a skein of geese flying past, their wings clapping.

He knew now that David was the key. There had to be a way to get him to come clean.

Josh glanced down at his watch. It was two o'clock. Then he remembered that David had an evening newspaper round which he usually began at four. Suppose he cycled over to his house and confronted him yet again? Was it worth the effort? He knew that it was a slender chance – but it was his only chance.

He couldn't face going home and he still wasn't in the least hungry, so he swam back to the bank and walked slowly down the towpath, kicking at a pebble, seeing the dust rise in the stillness of the afternoon.

As Josh wheeled his bike out of the shed Jack came round the corner. There was sweat on his forehead and upper lip, and his arms hung loosely by his sides.

"Where are you going?"

His voice was dull and hostile.

"Out for a ride."

"You haven't had your lunch."

"Don't feel like it."

Jack gripped Josh's handlebars, "I hope you're not being stupid."

"What do you mean?"

"Interfering."

Josh could feel the dead weight of his brother's enmity. He also had the strange feeling that Jack could see into his mind.

"I've told you what the trouble was."

"Yes."

"Now it's over."

"Why do you bully David so much?" Josh had instinctively sensed a tiny chink in Jack's armour and, for once, was bold enough to take advantage.

"Why do you keep repeating yourself?" But rather than sounding threatening, Jack now only seemed anxious.

Josh pressed home. "Because I don't understand."

"You're thick."

"Maybe. But I still don't get it. David's scared."

"He did a bad thing."

"Scared of *you*."

"I didn't want him dragging us all into it, involving Mum and Dad. Think of the row there would be." Strangely, there seemed to be an almost pleading note in Jack's voice that was wholly uncharacteristic.

Josh probed for the last time. "Is there anything you haven't told me?"

"Of course not."

"Please, Jack."

"What do you mean, 'Please, Jack'?" He was sneering now and once again he was the alien presence, the total stranger.

"Tell me what's going on—"

"You're an idiot." Jack was losing his temper again, but Josh knew he had to push him, whatever the consequences.

"There *is* something, isn't there? Something you haven't told me. Is it - is it something else you've done? Something—"

He was about to run through the other permutations when Josh saw that Jack's face was sweatier than ever and a little muscle was twitching at the corner of his eye.

"Shut up!" he said.

"If only—" Josh pressed on determinedly, but Jack shook the handlebars, the muscles in his forearms knotted and the veins in his wrists standing out.

"On your bike."

Josh cycled along the towpath as fast as he could, not afraid of pursuit but wanting to use up as much physical energy as possible. He had never felt so frustrated or so despairing as he wobbled past an indignant woman, his brakes screaming as he almost skidded into the river.

"You stupid child," she yelled, but Josh sped on, impervious to her rage. He had to get to David. He had to break him.

As he rode he remembered Jack towelling him down after the terrifying Mud Monster episode. He had cared, like he used to care. A sudden image came to Josh of Jack playing on the beach with him, making castle turrets from wet sand in a pail. He had showed Josh how to turn out the turret without the sand shape being damaged. They had knelt together, waiting for the tide to come in, watched it gradually knock the castle down, swirling about their knees as they witnessed the grand-scale demolition.

The Fletchers lived in a mews cottage with a pottery at the back, just off Henley High Street. As Josh rattled over the traffic-calming humps he glanced down at his watch. It was three-forty-five. He was early and he didn't want David to see him, at least not right away. Josh wanted to think, to try and work out what he was going to say. This time he must get the truth out of David, however hard that would be.

Next door to the Fletchers' rather ramshackle home was a garage that specialised in selling run-down second-hand cars, and a number of these were crowded on to the tiny forecourt. There didn't seem to be anyone around.

Josh leant his bike against the wall and wandered around among the cars. The hot tarmac looked as if it was going to melt at any moment into a black and glistening lake. The smell was almost overpowering and the sun beat down on him unmercifully.

The mews was so quiet that he had the strange impression that time was standing still. Josh looked again at his watch. The hands weren't moving. He stared at its face incredulously, then realised he had been mistaken. It *was* working after all.

A black cat with a white spot on its forehead darted towards him and rubbed itself against his bare leg with a piteous mewing sound.

"Go away," he hissed, but the cat continued to nuzzle him until David's door suddenly opened and he stood on the front step, pushing his bike out of the hallway, his face pale and drawn.

Josh ducked down behind one of the cars and watched him for a moment, still desperately thinking of what he was going to say.

"David." A big burly man with his long black hair in a pigtail stepped out behind him, and Josh recognised Mr Fletcher. His hands were covered in potter's clay, and he was wearing a stained apron.

David turned and a smile lit his face in a way Josh hadn't seen for a long time. He actually looked happy.

"Don't be late," said Mr Fletcher. "I'll have your tea ready for you." He leant over and kissed the back of David's neck and Josh felt a pang of jealousy. Dad was so remote. He hadn't kissed him since he was a young kid; the best they managed was a rather self-conscious handshake – and that rarely.

"Bye, Dad," said David.

With a wave, Mr Fletcher went back into the cottage and closed the door.

Still not knowing what he was going to say or do, Josh got up from behind the car. As he did so, the cat gave a squeal of protest and padded away.

"What is it?" David gazed at him fearfully, as if he must have brought bad news. "What's happened?"

"Nothing."

"Then why were you lying in wait for me?" His voice was shrill with protest.

"We've got to talk," Josh said doggedly.

"What about?"

"You *know* what about." He gazed curiously at David, sure that for a moment he had detected some kind of relief in him. David frowned and looked away.

"Why don't you just push off?"

He got· on his bike and tried to pedal away, but Josh grabbed the handlebars, just as Jack had grabbed his.

"Trust me."

"What about?" David looked completely trapped, but there was a stubborn line to his mouth.

"I won't give you away. I won't give anyone away. You *need* to talk to me." Josh tried to sound as forceful and as convincing as he could.

David paused and looked at him properly for the first time. "Yes," he said. "Yes, I do."

Josh stared at him in amazement. Was this the breakthrough?

"It's wicked." David's lower lip was trembling. The stubborn expression had gone.

Josh had never seen him look so hopeless.

"Wicked?" he echoed. "What do you mean?"

"You'll see."

"What *is* it? What are you trying to tell me?"

"I've got to do my round." David's face was set again.

"When will you finish?" Josh didn't want to argue with him or upset David in any way. He fully intended to coerce him, but knew he had to be patient.

"About six."

"You've got to meet me then."

David nodded, but didn't suggest anywhere. Then he said, "You'll have to come with me."

"On the round?"

He shook his head impatiently. "I'll show you." He was biting back a sob now. "But you're not to tell." He paused, staring down at Josh's hands. "I've got to know what to do."

"I'll help you," said Josh.

David looked up at him, the tears running down his cheeks. "I've got to know what to do," he repeated.

"Where shall we meet then?"

"At the pit."

"What pit?"

The shockwaves were spreading inside Josh to such

an extent that he could hardly contain himself.

"It's a quarry full of old cars. Down Beverley Lane. Do you know it?"

"I'll find it." It *was* the same place, exactly the same place.

"See you there about six."

Josh released David's handlebars.

"Please don't tell the others." David was becoming increasingly agitated, and Josh wondered whether he would actually be capable of doing the round.

"I won't tell anyone."

"Specially not Jack."

"I promise. You'll be there, won't you? You'll be at the pit. Don't let me down."

David shook his head and rode quickly away without looking back.

Josh cycled slowly through the sweltering streets of Henley. Trying to kill time, he prowled round the shops, eventually arriving at Riverside Books, his favourite haunt, where he knew he would be left in peace to browse. But as he turned the pages of a heavily illustrated book about Calcutta, the pit and its stacks of wrecked vehicles were mentally superimposed over each picture.

Suddenly, with mounting anxiety, Josh remembered yet again what Jack had said just after David had been sick on the *Moorhen*: "I'd run him back if only we had the—" Jack had broken off, gazing at Tom, Paul and

David fearfully, as if he had made a very serious blunder. Of course he had, thought Josh. The car. I'd run him back if only we had the – car. Did they drive one of the cars in the quarry? But even if they did – what was so wrong? What had happened to turn Jack into a monster?

Josh remembered his brother's ambition was to save up and buy some old banger of his own. He had taken on a number of part-time jobs but the pay had been poor and he and Tom now had plans to run a car-washing service.

Jack claimed that some boys he knew had saved half towards their first car and their parents had made up the difference, but Dad wouldn't do that. He had come from a poor background in South London and was determined that his children would "stand on their own feet". He had gone on to tell a sulky Jack that, "When the right time comes for you to have a car, you'll value it even more if you've paid for it all yourself."

Josh gazed vacantly at the pictures of street children in Calcutta. Why couldn't Dad have been more generous and said he would contribute something at least? Why was he always putting Jack down?

Jack certainly had his faults. He had always been an intolerant leader, someone who never suffered fools gladly, but he had also been generous, supportive and good fun to be with, particularly in those glorious "old" days when he had been so roughly kind to Josh, ordering him about, criticising him, but always fiercely loyal and protective.

So how had Secret Jack been born?

The lights flashed in the bookshop, and with mixed feelings of relief and anxiety Josh realised that it was five-thirty and if he cycled over to the quarry now he wouldn't have long to wait for David.

"Sorry I didn't buy anything," Josh said to the elderly man behind the counter. Anyway, he *did* buy books sometimes. Another gripe of Jack's was that Dad sometimes subsidised Josh for these, although he had refused to contribute to the car fund. "Books feed the mind," Dad had said uncompromisingly. "Cars just poison the atmosphere."

"That's all right," replied the bookshop owner. "I like to see you browsing."

"I was trying to think something out," Josh said with a burst of honesty, and then felt embarrassed.

"I didn't think you were that interested in Calcutta." The man was smiling.

"I *would* have been," said Josh guiltily.

"Sometimes one idea triggers off another."

Josh thought of the shanty towns in the book and the rotting hillside leading down to the mechanical hell of the quarry. There was certainly a similarity.

A slight haze hung over the pit and the smell was worse. Josh sat by the hole in the perimeter fence, watching a dusty worm burrow its way into the dry and powdery earth.

He felt alternately hot and cold, almost feverish, longing to see David cycling down the hill but at the same time tense with fear. How could the pit be connected with sabotaging Gerry's bike, Josh wondered. Had Gerry come down here to drive a car like the skinheads? Was his bike sabotaged while he was driving? The conjectures beat inside Josh's head, giving him a thundering headache, and his mouth was so dry that his thirst was fast becoming intolerable.

Then he saw the rat.

Chapter Seventeen

T HE CREATURE was enormous, with a long scaly tail, sunning itself on the other side of the fence, basking in the heat.

Josh stood up fearfully and banged on the wire. The rat scrabbled to its feet, boot-button eyes staring balefully at him for a moment before scampering away, heading for the sanctuary of a pile of rusting engines.

Josh shivered. What if the rat had been on his side of the fence, had brushed against him?

He walked over the rough ground to get a clearer view of the hillside. It was ten past six and there were no dust clouds and therefore no sign of David, only the waiting stillness he had experienced in the mews, except that this was much, much worse.

Slowly a burning resentment began to build up in Josh. Wasn't it bad enough that his brothers wouldn't confide in him, that he had lost Jack, that his parents were busy arguing between themselves? Now David wasn't going to arrive and Josh was never going to learn the secret after all. Life was incredibly unfair. Life was awful.

Out of the corner of his eye, Josh was sure he could see the rat emerging from under the carcass of an old truck, watching him in stealthy silence.

Then, with a rush of adrenalin, he saw the dust rising on the hillside. Someone was coming.

Josh felt a wave of nausea. Suppose the cyclist was Jack? He grabbed hold of his bike, preparing to make a dash for it directly he identified the rider. He began to tremble, certain now that his vengeful brother was on his way.

Then, to his relief and elation, through a break in the trees he could see David, cycling fast down the hill, his long hair streaming out behind him.

"You're late," said Josh accusingly.

"Sorry." David was sweating, the droplets all over his face and shining on his neck and arms. "Mr Robson kept me at the shop."

"What now?"

He got off his bike and leant it against the fence, looking round furtively at the same time. "Anyone here?"

"No."

"You sure?"

"You can see for yourself." Josh had had more than enough secrecy. "What are you going to show me?"

David stared at him with such concentrated misery that he knew he had to be much more patient.

"I'll help you," Josh tried to assure him. "Whatever it is, I'll help you."

"Will you?"

"I promise." He paused. "Are you really so scared of Jack?"

"He'd kill me if he knew what I was doing." David sounded utterly convinced.

"Jack wouldn't hurt you," Josh protested.

"You don't know him."

"Of course I do. He's my brother."

"You don't know your brother."

"Don't be such a pratt."

"He's changed." David paused and then said slowly, "We'll hide the bikes and then you'd better come with me, but you'll promise not to tell, won't you?"

Josh nodded. They pushed the bikes into a thick bush, then he followed David through the hole in the fence. Josh felt sick as he remembered the lurking rat.

The stacks of wrecked vehicles loomed above them, the rust glowing red in the afternoon sun. David's shoulders were hunched, as if he was forcing himself on.

Eventually they arrived at a huge pile of old tyres, a dark mountain against the deep blue of the sky.

David seemed to be concentrating very hard, his eyes downcast, hands clenching and unclenching. Then he turned round, his lips parted in a false grin.

"OK," he said. "I was winding you up, wasn't I?"

"Winding me up?" Josh was at first mystified and then incredibly angry. "Are you out of your mind?"

"There *isn't* any secret," he said. "Except about Gerry's bike. I mean that was it. I did wrong and I've been worried about not owning up. Jack kept telling me I mustn't."

"He kept threatening you as well." Josh tried to keep his temper under control but it was hard.

"Yes. He's a bit of a b-bully," David stuttered. "Anyway – you kept spying on us so I thought I'd lead you on a bit." His lips were still parted in that inane grin, but there was something behind it, a kind of wild despair.

"Is that all?" demanded Josh, the emptiness spreading inside.

"What else do you expect?" David began to shake with silent laughter as he stared up at the tyre mountain. Josh could hear the distant buzzing of flies and then he saw a cloud of them hovering a few yards up on the pile.

"You're crazy," he said.

David was still shaking, but his laughter wasn't silent any more. The hoarse sound seemed to burst from his lips, bubbling with rising hysteria.

"What the hell's going on?"

"I told you. It's a wind-up," he gasped. "A joke. I've fooled you. I've got to get back now." He swung away from the pile of tyres, but Josh grabbed his arm.

"You're not going anywhere."

"Get out of my way."

David tried to struggle but Josh held him tightly. There was something terribly wrong and there was no going back now. Not for either of them.

"Trust me," yelled Josh. "You've got to trust me."

David's whole body was rigid. "Jack will kill me."

"Don't be so stupid."

Again, David's eyes returned to the tyres. Then he seemed to make a sudden decision. Still gasping in the sultry heat, he bounded up the pile, his long legs flailing. "Come on then!"

Josh stared at him for a moment and then followed, quickly catching up as they climbed over the hot rubber mound.

"We were hoping it would catch fire of its own accord," yelled David mysteriously, "but it won't. So we'll have to do it. That was Jack's idea." He had paused on a small plateau among the tyres, almost parallel to the cloud of urgently buzzing flies.

Josh had a leaden feeling inside. "What are all those flies—" he began, but David ignored him, pulling at the tyres, laying them flat, dragging out more, until there was hardly any room to stand up. As he did so, Josh began to smell a sickly smell that was quite different from the other rotting material in the quarry.

David was shivering uncontrollably. Suddenly an eerie sound emerged from his fluttering lips – as if he was crying but on a high, shrill note. Then he stopped and there was silence.

Craning forward, staring through a gap in the tyres, Josh could see what he thought was a bundle of old clothes that were densely covered by the crawling black flies. But the smell, that awful smell, was much, much worse.

"Wicked," sobbed David. "It was wicked."

Chapter Eighteen

THE PLATEAU in the stack of tyres seemed to grow smaller as Josh edged closer, pushing at David, making him move over.

Then Josh saw the face. It was dark and matted with dry, caked blood, its eyes wide open, staring up at him. A fly, gorged by feasting, emerged drunkenly from under an eyelid.

David tried to start piling the tyres up again, but Josh wouldn't let him, grabbing at his wrist, gazing down as if hypnotised at the swirling black cloud, gagging at the strong sweet smell.

"I've got to cover him up again." David jerked his wrist away and Josh's stomach churned. Then he was violently sick over the side of the stack.

As David finished replacing the tyres, Josh stopped retching. Somehow they both climbed back to the ground, David in the lead, but glancing back anxiously, as if he wondered whether Josh was going to pass out and topple down on top of him.

They stood on the quarry floor for some time,

looking away from each other. Josh's throat was so dry he could hardly get the words out, but eventually he managed, "You found him?"

"No." David's voice was bleak.

Josh stared at him. He didn't want to understand.

"Actually," said David. "Actually we put him there."

There was a long, long silence.

Then Josh said, "You must be having me on."

"No."

Slow realisation dawned, however much his mind resisted the ideas that were forming in it. This was the secret. At last. "We've got to tell someone. We can't leave him there," said Tom's voice.

"What happened?" asked Josh, the shock waves still exploding inside him.

"Let's go away."

"You've got to tell me."

"I will. But I don't want to watch those flies."

"OK."

The two boys walked slowly down past the stacks until they came to a crane which stood etched sharply against the sun, the rust like the blood Josh had seen on the old man's face.

"Let's stop here," he said. He felt cold, despite the heat.

David leant against the hot metal.

"What happened?"

"Jack heard about the pit from some boys at

school." David spoke slowly and in a monotone, as if he had rehearsed the lines but they no longer had any meaning. "Heard about what you could do here."

"Drive the cars?"

"Yes." David was looking at a point on the ground. "How do you know?"

"I guessed," Josh replied uneasily. "Go on." He was still determined not to make the dreadful connection that he knew was waiting for him. It was like being on a roller-coaster with the ground coming up fast.

"We drove the cars. Lots of times. All four of us. This boy showed us how to start them up." He paused.

"Yes?"

"The old man. I think he lived here."

"You mean—"

"We were driving round a bend." David was panting now, gasping for air, as if he couldn't catch his breath. Then he spoke so softly that Josh could hardly hear: "We hit him."

"With the car?"

"Yes."

"You knocked him down?"

David nodded.

"You knocked him down in a car?" The cold was spreading further inside Josh, freezing his stomach, drying his mouth. He had always known the secret must be bad. But not this bad.

"He wasn't looking—"

"This isn't a motorway, or a race track." He was trying to cope by being angry now.

"I think he lived here. We found his shelter. He was a tramp, an old vagrant."

"But he was – he was a human being." Josh could hardly bring the words out. "You killed him."

David's face was working but there were no tears now.

"Who was driving?"

He was silent.

"Come *on*. Who was driving?"

"Jack."

"Jack killed him?"

"It was all of us."

"It was Jack."

A great shudder ran through David's thin frame.

"So you *didn't* sabotage Gerry's bike."

"No. That was – it was made up."

"You killed the old man. Then what?" Josh spoke slowly, unbelievingly.

"We didn't know what to do." He hesitated, stirring the dust with his foot.

"You should have called the police. It was an accident. They would have—"

"We shouldn't have been driving the car," David interrupted, but in the same monotone.

"Plenty of other kids did."

"Jack said that wouldn't help us. We'd be done for lots of stuff."

121

"But it was *still* an accident," Josh persisted. "Now it's worse."

"Yes."

"What did you *do*?" he bellowed, trying to keep the anger going and the despair out.

"We talked."

"Talked?"

"Just us four."

"So you talked?" Josh could hardly contain himself. He wanted to cry and hit somebody, something, all at the same time.

"In the end we decided to hide him."

"Just like that?"

David said nothing. After a while he continued. "We went home. Then Jack phoned."

"What did he want?" But Josh thought he knew.

"He didn't think – the old man was hidden properly, so we had to come back and cover him up again."

"You sure he was dead?" Suppose they had buried a man alive? It was an appalling thought.

"He was dead all right."

"How did you know?"

"It was obvious." David's voice shook. "Very obvious."

"Then what?"

"We went home again."

"Without even *thinking* of calling the police?"

"We were scared."

"It could have been sorted."

"We were scared," David repeated doggedly.

"And then?"

"Nothing. But I kept thinking about him." David cleared his throat. "I knew I – we – had to do something."

"Like go to the police at last?" demanded Josh. He was shaking with delayed shock.

"Yes."

"It was your idea?"

David nodded.

"But they wouldn't let you?"

He nodded again.

"Or at least Jack wouldn't."

David looked away.

"Why wouldn't he?"

"He was scared."

"Yes?"

"Like if your dad found out ..."

"So he bullied you into keeping quiet, despite the fact that you didn't want to." Josh's stomach heaved. He was aware of the irony. It wasn't the rat that revolted him now. It was his brother.

"I said we should go to the police. Lots of times." David was looking down again.

"Like that night on the river?"

David didn't reply. Then after a long while he said dully, "It's best to do nothing now. He was only a vagrant. He won't be missed."

"Is that what Jack told you to think, you stupid

zombie?" David shrugged, but Josh knew he had. Jack the stranger. Secret Jack. Not the brother he knew. Where was the old Jack? Was he as dead as the old man?

"You can't leave him here. He should be buried. Properly. Even if he was a vagrant." Josh tried to speak calmly, reasonably now, but his voice had a sob in it.

"We can't just take him to an undertaker, can we?" David gave him a stupid grin, not able to make any more decisions.

"You were right first time, Dave. You *do* have to go to the police. I'll come with you." They *had* to go, whatever the consequences. And the consequences were going to be dreadful.

"You said you wouldn't tell." David was rigid with anxiety, gazing at Josh as if he had betrayed him.

"*You'll* tell. It's the only way."

"Jack would kill me."

"Rubbish!"

"You can't know him."

"If you go to the police, they'll help you." Josh tried to find the patience to reassure him, to keep his own emotions in check for as long as he could.

"I won't do it." David was adamant, his features sullen and set, digging in.

"You must. What happens if he's discovered?" Everything seemed to be slipping out of Josh's grasp now, just as it always did. He realised the implications, knew what Mum and Dad would say, how badly they

124

would suffer. Jack knew that too.

"No one will know it was us."

"You might get grassed up," Josh warned him savagely.

"Who by? You?"

"If the body's found, there'll be a murder hunt." He was suddenly exhausted.

"Murder?" David gazed at him fixedly. "It wasn't murder."

"That's the way it could look."

"Jack won't let that happen." He seemed to have found some dogged confidence, elevating his tormentor into someone who was invincible. "He's going to torch the tyres."

"And the old man?"

"He's already dead."

"The police will still have you for it."

"They'll never know."

The conversation had become circular and desperately Josh tried another tack.

"You'll never live with it, Dave. You know you won't. And neither can I." At least Josh was sure of that.

"I *can't* go to the police."

Josh's mind raced. Suppose he *did* just leave it all alone? The old man was only a tramp after all. Only? He was a human being – not some dead animal to be burnt with the refuse.

"Someone's coming," said David, watching the spirals of dust on the hillside track.

Chapter Nineteen

"MIGHT BE those skinheads," said Josh, hoping that it wasn't Jack.

"Who?"

"Some guys I met down here."

"But you didn't say—" David broke off and gave him a hunted glance, but Josh knew what he was really concerned about. "Jack might be coming to torch the tyres. He said he'd do it soon. Maybe he followed me." David looked round hopelessly, but still didn't move as the dust cloud got lower on the hillside.

"We've got to hide," said Josh.

"Where?" asked David hopelessly.

Josh scanned the immediate vicinity, his panic rising, seeing nowhere that was possible. "There's an old bus over there. Let's try that," he said at last.

Jerkily they both began to run, but Josh had the awful feeling that, as if in a nightmare, he was running on the spot and getting nowhere.

Somehow they reached the bus, which still bore the faded legend THOMPSON'S TOURS. The vehicle had no wheels but was otherwise intact. Would the rat be in there waiting for him, wondered Josh with a surge of revulsion, or, worse still, a whole nest of them?

Inside, however, there was only darkness and weeds sprouting through the floor.

Josh and David crouched down, peering out through a dirt-encrusted window, hoping they were sufficiently concealed.

Slowly, relentlessly, Jack, Tom and Paul came into view, dumping their bikes on the other side of the fence, looking inexplicably carefree. Had the trio really arrived to burn a corpse?

Then, with disbelief, Josh saw his brother untie the petrol can from under his cross-bar and stride casually towards the stacks of old cars. He seemed calm, detached and confident. Josh could sense his relief. Beside him was Tom, as laid-back as ever.

Only Paul seemed uneasy, slouching behind the twins as they made their way past the coach without giving it a glance, and on down the stacks. For a moment Josh saw his brothers as avenging warriors, followed by their disgruntled servant, arriving to make a human sacrifice, except that the sacrifice had already been made.

The dark, blood-encrusted face of the old vagrant, with the fly crawling from under his eyelid, pushed its way into Josh's mind. It was all unbelievable. But it was no use cowering here; if he remained a silent witness to their secret he would be no better himself. He must stop the burning. As he watched the three strangers disappear from sight among the stacks, a terrible thought occurred to him. Would they burn him too? And David as well?

"They're going to torch the tyres," whispered David.

"They're going to burn the old man," replied Josh. He got up from his crouching position. "I can't let him do that."

"It's not just Jack—" David began.

"It is," Josh insisted. "If I can stop him, I can stop them all."

"Stay where you are," David whimpered. "He'll be terribly angry. Jack will kill me."

"Of course he won't." Josh was already hurrying down the rusty floor of the bus, scattering an army of ants. His change of mood was abrupt but he spoke with conviction. The old Jack must still be there. The old Jack would reach out, wouldn't hurt him. Josh *had* to be sure of that and, temporarily at least, he was.

"I'm coming with you," said David suddenly. "I can't be here on my own."

They ran down the stacks as hard as they could. I've got to stop him. I've got to stop him. The words pounded in Josh's head.

The car wrecks glinted and glimmered, the sunlight occasionally catching a metal surface, flashing at them like a warning. Jack's my brother, Josh repeated to himself. Jack loves me. Jack won't hurt me.

He could hear David panting behind him and ran on as fast as he could, trying to put everything into the physical effort so that he wouldn't be able to think of what was going to happen next.

Then they rounded the bend.

Jack was splashing petrol on the base of the tyres while Paul and Tom watched intently.

Josh tried to shout but his voice wouldn't work, and it was only after a supreme effort that he managed to rasp, "You've got to stop."

Jack paused, slowly put down the petrol can and turned round, the fixed smile back on his face. "What are *you* doing here?" He didn't sound exactly angry, just surprised, and Josh wondered if his brother was ill, if something had snapped in his mind.

"You've got to go to the police. You've got to stop what you're doing. Please, Jack. You know it isn't right."

His brother laughed. It was an unpleasant sound, strident and humourless. "Listen to him," he said. "Just listen to him."

"Did *you* give us away, David?" demanded Paul, moving towards his brother, bulkily menacing.

"Yes," said David, standing his ground, his voice surprisingly steady, as if he had found some courage at last. "I told him and he's right, we *should* go to the police. It's what I've been saying all along. It was only an accident. They'll understand."

Jack laughed again.

Tom cut through the long silence that followed. "It's best," he began slowly. "It's best we burn the tyres."

"Why?" asked Josh.

"We're going to make it not happen." Tom sounded far more childish than Josh had ever heard him, and knowing he only had David's weak support he felt very afraid.

"You can't do that," he said quietly.

"Why not?" asked Tom.

"He'll be missed." Josh desperately tried another ploy.

"Who by? He was only a tramp."

"He needs a proper burial."

"He's getting a cremation," said Jack. "That should be enough."

Paul suddenly aimed a wild swing at his younger brother with his fist, but he hardly connected and to everyone's surprise David kicked out, catching Paul on the leg. He howled with pain, clasping his ankle and staggering about on one foot. Had the situation not been so macabre the sight would have been funny, but in the circumstances it just seemed clownish, almost freakish.

"You fool," said Tom, expressing everyone's feelings. It was the only thing they could be united over.

Then Jack produced a box of matches and took one out, staring down at it, his face blank. "It'll be over in a few minutes. There won't be any evidence left. Then we can all walk away from this."

"I'll tell," Josh said. "You know I'll tell."

"You won't." There was an arrogant conviction in Jack's voice.

"It's for the best. It's got to be," said Tom.

But Josh was already running towards the tyre mountain, dodging his brothers, bounding up at it, climbing, scrambling, clambering until he was halfway up the pile. As he ran, he gasped for air, the buzzing sound stealing into his ears, growing increasingly loud.

Jack stared up at Josh for a while, shrugged, and then threw the match on to the petrol-soaked tyres.

Chapter Twenty

A FLAME leapt, followed by a thick cloud of dense black smoke, but Josh kept clambering on towards the flies that were still hovering above the grave of the old vagrant. He had no clear idea of what he was doing, beyond making some kind of protest, and when he looked down the smoke seemed to have lessened. Had the flame been smothered? If so, maybe the fire wouldn't take hold.

They were all looking up at him now, puzzled and curious, too shocked to be afraid.

"Get down," shouted Tom.

Paul, still clasping his leg, stared up at Josh, alarm spreading over his face. David watched silently.

"I'm going to light another match," said Jack. "See how you like that."

The black cloud was still buzzing amidst the thin skeins of drifting smoke, unanxious to leave. Josh began to choke. "I'm not coming down," he shouted. "Not till you decide to go to the police."

"You can't leave him up there," said Tom suddenly.

"I'm going up to get him."

"No, you're not," Jack replied. "I am." He put the match back in the box and glanced at the drifting smoke. "You wait," he yelled up at Josh. "You wait till I get you."

Jack began to climb.

The fire was only smouldering now, the smoke far less dense, and Josh knew that at least he had prevented his brother from lighting another match. But was this only a temporary diversion? Once Jack had beaten him up, would he get the fire going again?

Josh watched his brother climb, hand over hand, his face expressionless, effortlessly finding nooks and crannies among the tyres. Finally he reached Josh's level and slowly, very slowly, began to walk towards him.

For a while nothing happened as they faced each other, but eventually it was Josh who lost eye contact, no longer able to withstand Jack's hostility.

"If you tell anyone," he said quietly, "I'll kill you."

Josh's face whitened. "That's what you said to David," he muttered.

"Don't think I'm bluffing," Jack hissed, and Josh stepped back.

"Who are you?" Josh said involuntarily, staring at his brother so hard that he went out of focus.

"What are you talking about?" For a moment, Jack seemed thrown.

"You're someone else."

"Don't talk rubbish!"

"You're not my brother any more—"

Jack raised his fist as if to strike him, but Josh didn't back away.

"You're *not* my brother," he repeated in a dull voice. "He wouldn't do this. Just imagine what Dad would say if he knew—"

Jack gazed at him, looking trapped. He was the old Jack again.

"Get down," he said softly, and Josh knew the moment had passed.

"I'll come with you. I'll come with you to the police." He was pleading now, desperate to reach him again.

"Shut up." Jack shoved Josh hard in the chest and he fell back against the tyres. The smoke from below had increased, and as the acrid stench filled his lungs, Josh began to choke.

"I'm going to tell. I *have* to," he gasped. They were both choking now.

"Then we'll stay here together until you change your mind."

Jack was standing over Josh, straddling him with his legs as the smoke increased, the dark billows searing their throats and making their eyes water.

Josh could hear Paul and David shouting below, their voices indistinct.

"Let me up!" gasped Josh.

"Not till you promise not to tell."

"I can't."

"Then we – we'll – stay – here—"

"Let – me – up."

Josh grabbed Jack's legs, but they seemed to be made of iron.

The smoke was smothering them, but Jack still stood firm and Josh wrenched at his legs again and again without the slightest effect.

Then, suddenly overcome by a fit of coughing, Jack staggered and Josh was able to roll away until he reached the edge of the plateau. He scrambled for a handhold but found none, pitching over the drop.

Fortunately the tyres were more erratically stacked on the other side and Josh bounced from layer to layer until he came to rest on another plateau.

He lay there, bruised and choking, watching a huge flame dart up behind the tyres, losing itself in an even denser pall of smoke, a spiralling dark serpent, shooting up to the innocent blue of the cloudless sky.

"Jack!" he screamed. "Jack, where are you?"

Then he saw his brother bounding down the stack towards him, the smile slashing his features like a raw wound, an awful slit that seemed to get wider as he came nearer. Josh rolled again, somehow got to his feet, and began to jump from level to level, with his brother gasping behind him.

Josh tumbled on to the hard, flinty surface of the quarry, picked himself up and began to run, but he knew he was going in the wrong direction, darting back along the stack of cars, the scrap piled high on either side, cutting off any possible form of escape.

Josh pounded along until he realised that he could no longer hear Jack's footsteps or the sound of his ragged breathing. He glanced fearfully over his shoulder to see that the long path between the stacks was empty. His brother seemed to have completely disappeared.

He paused, waited for Jack to jump out of some hiding place, but there was no sign of him, the quarry deadly quiet except for the now more distant crackling of the fire and the noxious smell of burning rubber.

Josh realised he had completely lost his bearings and had no idea where he was. He waited, trying to make up his mind what to do.

Then he heard the familiar spluttering of a reluctant engine, whirring and whining again and again and then abruptly bursting into raucous, roaring, menacing life.

At first Josh wasn't sure where the sound was coming from, and as panic overcame him he began making little darting runs, first in one direction and then another. Then an old battered and doorless Rover came round the bend with Jack at the wheel, gunning the engine, heading straight for him, the gash smile on his lips, his eyes blank, devoid of any pity, devoid of any emotion at all.

There was nowhere to go except to climb the nearest stack, but this time it was much more difficult, for Josh would have to get to grips with piles of rusting vehicles rather than the much more climbable layers of tyres. He sprang on to the roof of a crushed Volvo, grabbed the bonnet of a VW, hauled himself over a battered Mini and on to the flat back of a small truck.

Meanwhile, Jack waited below in the Rover, its engine idling, waiting to see which escape route Josh would take, ready to cut him off.

As he managed to straddle the topmost vehicle, Josh paused and gazed down. Jack was grinning up at him, his hands lightly gripping the steering wheel. The game was on and, like all games, Josh was sure his brother would win. But he was also sure his brother was ill. The secret had become too much for him.

Despair swept him. If he climbed down the other side, Jack would be there before him. If he stayed where he was, Jack would wait. There were no rules. Only penalties.

Josh gazed across the stack. The other side was considerably steeper, the wrecked vehicles much more closely bonded together, and any descent would be like climbing down an almost sheer cliff. Anyway, what was the point of trying if Jack was going to be waiting for him at the bottom?

For a few seconds, Josh stayed where he was, the indecision numbing his mind, making him unable to move.

Below him, Jack revved the Rover triumphantly. Where were the others, Josh wondered. What were they doing? Trying to put out the fire? But what with? Or were they just standing there, watching the flames and smoke take hold?

The pall was denser now, blotting out the sky, and Josh gazed down at the stranger that was his brother, staring into his eyes, searching for even a trace of the old Jack he had loved and looked up to, but seeing only a murderous stranger.

He stared down again at the sheer side of the stack. With the terror of sudden vertigo, he felt the ground drawing him. Turning his back on the drop, Josh lay down flat and threw a leg over the abyss. Slowly he began to climb down.

At first he made good progress for just below him was the overhanging, crazily twisted roof of a post office van. Josh lowered himself on to it from the flattened car above, but when he glanced down he couldn't see any kind of foothold on the smooth-sided truck below. The vehicle was lying on the side of another truck which lay on top of another and another and yet another. But that wasn't all. Underneath the stack, the bottom of the quarry fell away into a shallow dip that was full of scaffolding and rusty metal. Josh shuddered. The long, sharp poles reared up at him, and he knew that if he fell he would impale himself.

Then Josh heard the Rover rattle into life, the deadly roar of its clapped-out engine shattering the silence. Jack was coming. He searched for a grip on the side of the truck but found nothing. Blindly lowering himself over the edge, he grabbed the bumper of the post office van.

Suddenly his foot slipped and he was falling again,

grazing his hand and then his shins, until he came to an abrupt halt, clinging with both hands to the axle of the truck above him.

Josh gazed down. He wouldn't be able to hang on for long.

There was a screech of brakes and he guessed the Rover had come to a halt somewhere to the right of the stack he was on, although he couldn't actually see it. He smelt the stench of the exhaust fumes and then heard Jack's feet crunching over glass and what sounded like metal.

"You idiot!" His voice was sharp, full of contempt. "Get back up."

"I can't."

"If you try and come down, you'll kill yourself."

"I can't move." Josh feebly straightened his arms and tried to grip the metal harder, but it was slippery with oil and he knew he wouldn't get any purchase. Numbly, he watched the pall of smoke thicken again and then darken the blue sky more densely. He felt detached, almost disembodied, except for the pain in his arms.

"Hang on," said Jack sharply. "I'll get you out of there. Stay where you are."

"I'm not going anywhere," he said, trying to joke.

"You'd better not try." Josh couldn't work out whether there was hostility or concern in Jack's voice. Then his brother said, "If I get you down, will you promise not to tell?" He sounded childish now.

Josh was silent. "I can't," he said at last, the words almost wrenched from him.

"Then you'll stay there," said Jack angrily.

"I'll fall," Josh whimpered.

"Promise."

I could break the promise, thought Josh. I could easily break it. He knew, however, that he couldn't and realised the final test had come, not so much of his own bravery but of his brother's love for him. He wanted to bring the old Jack back, and Josh knew that this was the only way.

"I can't promise."

"You mean you'd rather fall?"

"I mean I won't promise."

Jack began to walk slowly away.

"Where are you going?" A wave of panic passed through Josh, leaving behind cold fear.

"Away."

"You can't," he yelled. "Suppose I fall?"

"That'll be your bad luck."

There was nothing in his brother's tone to suggest that he was going to be merciful.

"You *can't* leave me here. You can't do that, Jack."

"I can."

Josh looked down and the scaffolding poles seemed to loom jaggedly up at him. He shouted his brother's name several times, but after a while he realised with total despair that Jack had gone away and that somehow they had both failed the test.

Chapter Twenty-one

THE SWEAT ran down Josh's forehead and into his eyes. He wouldn't look down again in case he fell, but already his hands were beginning to slip on the greasy axle. Jack couldn't leave him. But he had. He simply didn't care whether he lived or died.

His arms were trembling and he felt a band of nausea tighten in his stomach. Was he going to be sick? If he was, he would lose his grip and fall straight on to the jagged metal.

"Jack," he yelled. "Jack?"

There was no reply.

"Jack? Are you there?" There was a sob in Josh's voice now, but he could only hear the gentle rumbling of the burning tyres.

Josh's arms were shaking so hard that he knew he couldn't keep his grip any longer. Cramp had begun in his left foot, giving him such a thrusting pain that he could hardly bear it.

"Jack!" he yelled and then listened intently for an answering cry, but there was only the dull crackling of flames. Dizziness overcame Josh, yet he still hung on, not calling but saying Jack's name in his head silently, over and over again. You're my brother, he thought. You loved me. You've *got* to help me.

Then Josh felt a tiny surge of hope, for he was sure he hadn't heard the sound of the Rover's engine. Jack hadn't driven off. So where was he? And where were the others?

Time crawled by. Josh watched some kind of small flying insect hover over his left wrist and then disappear into the darkness underneath the truck.

Then he felt something alight on his underarm, creeping down his bare flesh until he could see the wasp wandering over his wrist. Could he still hang on if it stung him? Even now the wasp was tickling his fingers.

Miraculously, Josh didn't let go, but the cramp in his foot was getting worse and his grip just that little bit weaker.

Metal City. Josh closed his eyes against it all, the nausea and giddiness getting worse. The place seemed to be taking over his mind now; galvanised pole people spat rust, iron stick insects clattered together, scaffolding figures leapt in clanging dance.

The city smelt of oil and petrol and exhaust fumes and burning rubber. It was evil, like Jack. It buried its victims and soon he would be crushed in its metal arms. Josh saw again the dead face of the old man, the dried blood in his matted hair.

Click, clack, went the voice of the city. We're waiting for you. A skeletal steel bird scraped past in the grey metallic sky of his mind, and a tin man marched triumphantly across his imagination until his rusty joints seized up. The steel nightmare continued. The city scraped iron-filing fingers.

"Josh!" came the familiar voice.

Metal men paraded the air, probing at him, wrenching Josh away from the axle which now seemed to be revolving, creating a film of grease. The machinery cranked on. Hammers beat in his feet, pistons in his eyes and all around him was the clamour of copper drums.

"Josh!" The voice was much more agitated now.

A fretsaw worked on his wrists, rocks bounded off his mind, ball bearings ground in his ears, the wasp's buzz was an oxyacetylene cutter, and a silver-plated gong sounded...

"Josh – for Christ's sake!"

He opened his eyes to see Jack's face hanging over the post office van at an incredible angle.

"You're flying," said Josh in wonder. It was a miracle. A metallic miracle.

"Tom and Paul have got my ankles. David's below you but don't look down."

Josh didn't, but his brother's face appeared to be going round and round.

"Don't let go. At least not till I tell you. Got it?"

Josh nodded.

143

"They're going to lower me down, so shut up, do what you're told and listen. I can just grab your wrists, but you *don't* let go until I say. Do you understand?"

Josh closed his eyes against the impossibility of it all.

"Open your eyes," Jack yelled. "*Do* you understand? Open your eyes!"

Josh opened them.

"OK." Jack was breathing in short gasps. "I'm coming."

Slowly he was lowered down by his ankles, wiry wrists dangling just above Josh.

"I've still got to tell," he whispered.

"I know," said Jack. "Now, shut up. I'll get you out of this, but you must do exactly what I say. Are you listening?"

Josh nodded.

"I think I can just reach you, but you're not to let go yet. Whatever you do."

"I won't."

Suddenly Josh could feel his brother's strong fingers locked around his wrists, tightening, tightening, and then clamping rock solid.

"Let go *now*!"

It was easy. Like flying. Rusty tambourines crashed in the metal city below, kettle drums screamed.

Slowly, very slowly, Josh was dragged to safety, until he was back on the roof of the post office van which nestled so snugly against the other vehicle on which Tom and Paul were lying flat out, having hung on to Jack's ankles for so long.

For a while they all lay exhausted, and then Josh felt himself being dragged to his feet.

"We did it!" yelled Paul. Suddenly he was no longer a malicious clown but a friend.

"You OK?" Tom wasn't laid-back any more. He was grinning with affection.

"He's great." Jack ruffled Josh's hair. "He's absolutely great."

"What's happening?" came David's anxious voice from below.

"You tell him," said Jack.

"I'm safe!" bellowed Josh. "I'm absolutely and completely safe." Never had he felt so exultant. Never had he felt so happy.

David's cheer from below was faint but relieved.

As they clambered down the stack, sirens began to wail and their elation evaporated.

"Someone must have seen the smoke," said Jack. "Let's go."

David came running round the corner to join them as they scrambled down the stack and raced for the hole in the wire fence. Grabbing their bikes, they began to pedal furiously, heading for the hillside, straining every muscle to try and put as much distance between them and the pit as possible.

Josh could still feel Jack's steel fingers on his wrists.

How could he ever have thought his brother would kill him?

There was no attempt at pursuit. When Josh glanced over his shoulder he could see that fire engines had arrived at the quarry and the firemen were already cutting away at the wire while hoses were being uncoiled and a hydrant desperately sought. Meanwhile the ever thickening black smoke rolled noxiously up into the sky, the occasional little tongue of flame darting here and there.

The old man's funeral pyre was complete.

The five of them paused gasping at the top of the hill, leaning on their handlebars, their hearts pumping.

"We're going to the police station," panted Josh. "Aren't we?"

There was a long silence. Then Jack said, "Don't be a fool." He gazed down at the smoke. "No one's ever going to find him now, are they?"

"That's right," said Paul, following Jack's lead. "What's the point of getting into trouble for nothing?"

Exhausted and numbed, Josh couldn't believe that all his efforts had been in vain, that they still weren't going to own up. Already Jack was jumping on to his bike, giving the usual lead to the others to do the same.

Somehow, Josh knew he had to stop them. "You can't go," he said weakly. "You've *got* to tell."

Jack turned back to him, his expression patient, as if he was explaining to an idiot. "There's nothing to worry about, Josh. It's over."

"You killed someone."

"Accidentally."

"You've got to tell," Josh repeated woodenly.

Jack sighed, but he remained kind, almost calm. "It would kill Mum and Dad – Tom knows that – and what about Mr Fletcher?"

The others remained silent. Jack was the spokesman and Josh was finally at a loss for words.

Jack began to ride away and the others followed.

"Aren't you going to the police?" Josh bellowed at David. "Aren't even *you* going?"

"Jack's right," he replied blandly. "There's no point."

Josh pedalled as hard as he could, squeezing past the others on the narrow track and catching up with Jack. "You've *got* to go to the police," he shouted.

Jack skidded to a halt, his face twisted in rage, his patience over, and Josh only just managed not to crash into him. His brakes screaming, he steadied his bike while the other three did the same.

"It was an accident." Jack's face was rigid and pale under his tan. "Just an accident." He spoke wearily, as if he, too, could hardly take any more. "Now it's over."

"You should have told the police directly it happened," yelled Josh.

"Well, we didn't," replied Jack firmly. "We took the decision not to."

"It was wrong," bellowed Josh. "It was wrong – wasn't it, David?"

But David didn't reply.

"OK," sobbed Josh. "OK, then."

"What does that mean?" Jack glared at him.

"*I'll* tell."

"On your own brother?"

"Yes."

"You know what that would mean, don't you? That we'd all go into youth custody. Maybe we'd go to prison for life."

"It's better than covering it up," said Josh. "Look what happened when you did."

The others were silent; it was as if they didn't exist. The battle of wills was between Jack and himself.

"What happened then?"

"You were all scared out of your minds. Trying to keep the secret. It must have been awful."

For a second, Jack hesitated. Then his eyes hardened again.

"It's all over," he said. "I'm sorry about it."

"It? It was a him."

"I'm sorry about *him*. He just stepped out in front of the car. I couldn't avoid him."

"The police will understand it was an accident. That you tried to avoid him."

"They won't." There was a shut-in look in Jack's eyes.

Josh knew what he had to do. He would *have* to tell on them. But maybe not to the police – to Dad. He looked at his watch. Eight. Dad would be home by now. Josh would tell them both. His parents would know what to do.

Josh moved so fast that Jack was momentarily taken by surprise as he pushed his bike past his. "I'm going to Dad," he said, jumping on the saddle and pedalling hard again.

"You're not," yelled Jack. "You're *not*!"

They were all after him like a pack of wolves, yelling and cursing, standing up on their pedals, wanting to hunt him down. When Josh fearfully glanced back he could see that even David was one of the pack, his eyes glinting with the same rage.

Somehow Josh stayed just ahead, the scruffy little lane joining the main road now, cars hooting as the five of them careered out on to the tarmac, David and Paul two abreast at the back, Tom in the middle and Jack at the front, only yards from Josh's back wheel.

He had to put more distance between them, had to stop them overtaking or cutting him off, but already Josh's calf muscles were aching and his legs seemed filled with lead. He tried to brush the sweat out of his eyes but it kept streaming down in ever growing quantities.

Now the pace was even more furious as the gradient went downhill. The road was coming into town, the streets building up, and the sudden corner, familiar as it was, had a sharp, steep camber that was difficult to steer round at such speed. Josh just managed to stay on but Jack didn't.

Losing control, his bike brushed the kerb and he went flying over the handlebars, his head hitting the solid metal of a post box.

Brakes screamed as the others slewed to a halt amidst the sound of hooting vehicles from both sides of the road.

Josh skidded, stopping his bike in a haze of gritty dust. Through it he saw the post box with Jack lying against it. The paintwork was already scarlet red but now there was a deeper, darker substance dripping down its shiny surface.

Josh knelt down by his brother while Tom, Paul and David stood awkwardly, almost as if in some embarrassment, at the front of the gathering crowd. It was still between the two of them, Jack and Josh, as if they had to share the responsibility for what had happened.

Then more blood shot from Jack's mouth. He's broken, thought Josh, broken inside.

"Jack?"

His brother gazed up at him, through unfocused eyes.

"Tell him," he whispered. "Tell Dad."

"Are you—"

"I'm sure."

"Someone's calling the ambulance," said Tom, kneeling down beside them. "It won't be long —" He suddenly sounded like Dad – brisk and reassuring, as if he had grown up very quickly.

"I want Mum," muttered Jack. "Please. Get Mum."

The blood was running more freely down his chin now and the glazed look in his eyes was increasing.

Paul began to cry and David stared down unblinkingly.

"Jack," whispered Tom. "Oh, Jack."

They were kids all the time, thought Josh. Just frightened kids.

Chapter Twenty-two

THEY TOOK turns talking to Jack as he lay in the hospital bed, wired up to so many tubes that they could hardly recognise him. He had slipped into a coma as the ambulance took him away from the scene of the accident, and had slid deeper into unconsciousness as the hours passed.

Josh felt numb as he stood beside his father, watching the tears slide down his cheeks.

The doctors had told Dad and Mum that Jack might have brain damage and they couldn't at this stage say how severe it was. Nevertheless, they wanted his family to talk to him as much as possible, to try every means of stimulation. It was hard, talking to someone who didn't respond.

Friends had recorded tapes which were played over and over to him and one of his favourite rock musicians had already sent him a message on a cassette. But he didn't hear. Jack just lay on the bed, flat on his back, his eyes half shut, his mouth slightly open. No longer the old Jack, nor the secret Jack. Empty Jack instead.

"He might be able to hear you," one of the doctors had explained. "Don't say anything that you wouldn't want him to know."

Tom had told Dad and Mum what had happened to the old vagrant, and although they were deeply shocked it was nothing to the shock that they had received as a result of Jack's accident.

They had, however, told the police, who had interviewed Tom, Paul and David, who had all confessed and been totally cooperative. The burnt remains of the old man's body had been found and taken away and the police had said that they were "actively considering the situation".

Josh had also been interviewed, and had tried to explain that the twins and the Fletchers had not meant to be so wicked. "That's for us to consider," the officer had told him kindly but firmly. "You just stick to the facts."

And he had.

As a result, Josh felt a crippling sense of responsibility, and no amount of common sense from his parents made any difference.

"If I'd kept quiet," he had told Mum, "Jack wouldn't have been hurt."

But she had shaken her head. "You did the right thing, Josh. You've *got* to believe that."

He found it hard.

The Tyler family divided into rotas in an attempt to

153

stimulate Jack. This afternoon it was Josh, Mum and Dad's turn.

They worked as a team, talking to him quietly, often repeating themselves. Eventually Josh sat beside the bed on his own, while his parents stood over by the window, looking out. He turned to watch them for a few seconds and noticed they were holding hands.

Then Josh gazed back into Jack's blank eyes and began to talk to him quietly.

"Dad and Mum are getting on better now. I think you've brought them together again." His voice broke as he stroked Jack's fingers that were rigidly clasped together. Then he tried to recover himself. "Things will be different when you get better. You *will* get better. I know you're in there. I know you're there, Jack."

Mum and Dad came over to join him and, to Josh's surprise, Mum softly began to sing an old lullaby Josh remembered from when he was a baby. She must have sung it to Jack and Tom as well.

> *"I had a little nut tree,*
> *Nothing would it bear*
> *But a silver nutmeg*
> *And a golden pear.*
>
> *The King of Spain's daughter*
> *Came to visit me,*
> *And all for the sake*
> *Of my little nut tree."*